THE EMOTIONAL MENU

WHAT JUST HAPPENED?

Uncovering the hidden truths behind life's puzzling moments through storytelling.

LUZ MARIA VASQUEZ

izziocity
www.izziocity.com
Atlanta, Georgia

WHAT JUST HAPPENED?

CONTENTS

ACKOWLEDGEMENTS

To all my beloved children

Jacob, my spiritual mentor.

Hector, the breadwinner and material provider.

Adriana, my business coach and the inspiration
behind my decision to write.

Rachael, a powerful and intelligent soul.

Marco, a wise and quiet loner, like me, whose untold story I yearn to hear.

In memory of my late mother, who lived 92 full years.

To Martha, my health guru sister, and my generous and wise boss.

A special acknowledgment to my daughter-in-law, my steadfast companion in all
adventures.

To Anne, my boss - who believed in me, trusted my abilities, and stood by
me in tough moments. Her leadership, wisdom, and kindness have guided my path,
and I'm deeply grateful for her support.

Gratitude to readers and storytellers who dared to share their tales.

I am proud of each and everyone of you, keep telling your stories!

Much love to all!

INTRODUCTION

What Just happened?

As a child, life seemed simple and light, despite having no toilets, no running water, and no electricity.

Then one day, my family decided to migrate to the USA. I was 14 years old when the journey began. We stationed ourselves in Tijuana, at the US-Mexico border. Each sibling awaited their turn to cross. The cost to cross was high, and there were many of us. My mom and two little sisters went first. When it was finally my turn, my mother insisted that I be accompanied by my big brother for my safety.

However, as we were crossing, we got separated. I ended up in the hands of one man after another, men who were put in charge of my safety. It was a dangerous position to be in, and I had to fight them off to avoid being abused.

When I finally arrived at my destination, the home I found myself in was beautiful and welcoming at first. However, I soon had to fight for my safety almost every night as the abuse slowly became unavoidable. I was in a foreign country, struggling with a new language and culture, and again trying to survive my environment.

When I turned 18, I had my first child, a boy. To make life easier, I agreed to a loveless marriage, which eventually ended in divorce. I married again and soon divorced again. By this time, I had four more children: two girls and two boys.

Later, I found myself married for a third time, which also ended in divorce. Now, as a single mother working as a waitress to make ends meet, life began to feel overwhelming. I started questioning if there was a way to make it lighter. I reflected on my situation, always wondering why life felt so heavy. Feeling uncertain about the future, I found myself plagued by doubts and insecurities. I kept asking if there could be a way to lighten life up.

Then, at my lowest point, something miraculous happened that opened my eyes to question everything in my life. I was sitting there, confused, feeling trapped in a cage, thinking about the moment when my children and late husband abandoned me. I felt so hopeless and in despair. To feel better, I tuned in to my favorite speaker. He said something that shook me: "If I want to be free, I got to be me, and if I want to be me, I got to be free."

Those words made me jump out of my seat, because I knew right then and there that at some point in my life, I had lost my identity. I had lost the sense of who I was.

In my head, I heard a voice: "I am lost, trapped in a maze with no way out. I am lost. But lost in what?" I started putting my life on paper as if I were deciphering a code, writing down and questioning all the choices I made and experiences I had.

The deeper I explored, the more I saw where, when, and how I lost myself in my own unresolved emotions, limiting beliefs, and fears that were contributing to moments of lost control.

I discovered my unresolved emotions had me constrained. As a child, I created beliefs such as "I am unworthy, I am unwanted, I don't belong," and "I am not enough."

When these beliefs get triggered by anything unknown, the 'what just happened' moments show up without warning—moments of sudden confusion where I feel disoriented. These moments leave me momentarily puzzled or in disbelief, trying to make sense of what just happened and why I momentarily lost my emotional stability.

In identifying the triggers, I was able to see what I was lost in—my own unresolved emotions, made up of beliefs that were not true but were created by me at a young age, which had led me to become a fearful person, afraid to act and afraid to speak.

The more I discovered, the lighter I felt. The lighter I felt, the more I could accomplish, and the more I could accomplish, the happier I became. Life was becoming easier and easier.

By the time you finish reading 'What Just Happened', I hope you'll have a deep understanding of what triggers are and how to identify them.

Understanding your triggers is a vital step in uncovering the beliefs you invented about yourself as a child. These hidden beliefs often cause unresolved emotions to resurface.

Remember, this journey is about discovering and healing those parts of yourself, and I'm here with you every step of the way.

I can't wait to see your weight reduction, years dropping, looking younger, finding your soulmate, creating new relationships, getting along with friends, family, coworkers, or whatever it is that you most desire in your life.
The possibilities are endless. This book, What Just Happened, is not merely a collection of words bound by paper; it is a sacred invitation to embark on a journey of self-discovery and empathy. Within these pages, you'll find reflections of your own joys and sorrows, mirrored in the lives of fellow travelers.

With Empathy and Love,

Luz Maria Vasquez

I

SEARCHING FOR ANSWERS

CHAPTER ONE:
A TIRELESS SEARCH FOR ANSWERS

Have you or someone you know ever experienced a moment where you are left puzzled, CONFUSED? Unsure of WHAT just occurred?

Some of us, at one point or another, have been left in confusion, perplexed; in an instance of confusion, we are faced with complex emotions and struggle to comprehend the puzzling situation. The mind is actively engaged, trying to figure out the mysteries of the circumstances, much like attempting to solve a complicated puzzle with crucial pieces missing.

These moments can be referred to as 'perplexing moments' or 'baffling situations.' Or, simply put, it is a 'What Just Happened' moment.

To illustrate this point, let us examine the characters Lucy, Mia, and Johnny.

One beautiful morning, they were sitting in a cozy café, engaged in friendly conversation under the comforting rays of sunlight. The ambiance of the café was delightful, resonating with the cheerful chatter of other patrons and the inviting aroma of freshly brewed coffee. Positioned around a round table, the friends savored their drinks, immersed in joyful conversation. But then, out of nowhere, Mia got up and abruptly walked away without uttering a word.

Completely unaware of the reason behind Mia's sudden departure, Lucy and Johnny exchanged glances at each other and simultaneously exclaimed, 'What just happened?' Lucy, concerned for Mia, took it upon herself to search for her and unravel the meaning of 'What just happened.' Eventually, Lucy found Mia alone in her car, tearfully crying.

Lucy approached her and asked, 'Mia, what just happened?' Through sobs and a trembling voice, she responded, "What happened? Don't you know? You threw a party and invited all of our friends, except me. I was left out!"

Why did that affect Mia so much? Why was she offended so badly? What is behind all this and what are the exact words in that conversation that triggered the emotions to be stirred up? These questions and and more will be answered through the reading of the publication.

It is evident that Mia is likely grappling with negative emotions or negative thinking. It is common for many of us to struggle with negative thoughts and emotions, which often stem from the internal dialogues we engage in within our minds. Often, these dialogues consist of self- deprecating phrases such as:

· I am not smart enough.
· I am not deserving.
· I am unlovable.
· I am inadequate.
· I am unworthy.
· I am unwanted.

These negative beliefs seem endless, weighing us down with sadness, unhappiness, and a lack of motivation.

Over time, they can erode our self-worth, harm our relationships, and chip away at our confidence and self-esteem. In social settings, these feelings can lead to awkwardness and embarrassment, gradually pulling us away from meaningful connections.

Over time, they drain our energy, leaving us exhausted and unwell, often driving us to seek comfort in ways that may not truly heal. How do people typically cope with these overwhelming feelings and negative thoughts?

Some might turn to overeating or binging, while others may distract themselves with phone games or movies. Still, others might choose to sleep all day, take solitary walks in the park, or isolate themselves in a dark room.

In more extreme cases, individuals may resort to harmful practices such as relying on pills, alcohol, or drugs to escape their sorrows and feelings of inadequacy. While finding relief from discomfort, emotions, or demanding situations can feel great, it is often short-lived as these feelings tend to resurface when we resume our regular activities. This cyclic pattern can indeed feel like a vicious cycle, as the negative emotions seem to repeat themselves.

One day, I started noticing that, from time to time, I was experiencing awkward moments, grappling with anxiety or distress, or simply caught in a cycle of negative thoughts. It became clear to me that I was not alone in this — many of us face similar discomfort.

These emotional disruptions began affecting my daily routine, preventing me from taking action and limiting my ability to perform at my best. They also held me back from accomplishing my goals, building meaningful relationships, finding happiness, and maintaining my health.

As I realized that merely being aware of these challenges was not enough, I began asking myself, what is the remedy? What path should I take to finally gain control over my life?

Take a moment to pause and reflect on your own life. Stress is affecting which areas? Can you pinpoint specific moments that trigger emotional distress? Think about how you typically cope with these challenges.

Take some time to consider your responses, and jot down your thoughts. As you reflect, try to answer the question as if it just happened:

"WHAT JUST HAPPENED?"

_____
_____
_____
_____
_____
_____
_____

"HOW DO YOU COPE WITH IT?"

My insatiable thirst for answers, an intense longing or craving for knowledge and understanding, remained persistent, consuming my thoughts and actions day after day.

After a long period of searching, one day, something amazing happened. As I listened to a great speaker, Bob Proctor, who was a Canadian self-help author and lecturer. Someone I consider a mentor, their words caught my attention, and it was as if a lightbulb switched on. In that moment, I finally discovered the direction I had been searching for in my journey.

What was it? What made this moment so special? It was a phrase that stuck with me. The speaker profoundly declared, 'If I want to be free, I've got to be me. And if I've got to be me, I've got to be free.' Upon hearing those insightful words, I had a moment of realization. It became clear to me that in order to truly be myself, I must become free.

As I ponder on those worlds, another question arose within me: free from what, or free of what? Then, he explained how our past experiences bind us and restrain us from authentically expressing our true identity. I wondered, how can I truly express who I am if I am bound, restricted, and constrained? What does it mean to be bound, restricted and constrained; and how can one attain the freedom to access their authentic self?

To truly know oneself goes beyond knowing one's name, origin, or family background—it requires a deeper journey of self-discovery and understanding. Genuine self- knowledge involves exploring the core of our humanity, delving into our thoughts, feelings, values, and identity. By examining how we respond to emotions like stress, joy, or anxiety, and by reflecting on our behaviors, beliefs, and attitudes, we uncover valuable insights about our character and personal growth.

This deeper understanding enables us to make choices aligned with our values, aspirations, and desires. It allows us to break free from limiting patterns and create positive changes in our lives.

By recognizing our strengths, weaknesses, and triggers, we cultivate self- awareness and resilience, empowering ourselves to navigate challenges effectively.

Additionally, knowing ourselves fosters empathy and a deeper understanding of others. As we explore our emotions and reactions, we become more attuned to the experiences of those around us, building healthier, more compassionate relationships.

In essence, self-discovery leads to personal growth and transformation. It liberates us from being trapped in cycles of limitation, enabling us to live authentically, make intentional choices, and connect meaningfully with others.

Understanding the essence of our humanity reveals the motivating forces behind our actions and behaviors, offering clarity on what truly sustains and influences us.

FIRST ENCOUNTER
WITH LIFE'S STRUGGLES

Before life's challenges took hold, we were free—free of worry, concerns, judgment, and assessments. From birth, we are seen as whole, complete, and perfect beings.

However, as we grow and experience life, something changes. Disappointments, setbacks, and failures begin to shape us, slowly chipping away at that initial sense of freedom and wholeness.

These experiences can come from many sources—unmet expectations, failures, or negative encounters—and they have the power to alter how we see ourselves. Over time, they create a sense of incompleteness, as if a crucial part of us is missing. Like a puzzle with a missing piece, our self-perception becomes fragmented, leaving us searching for what feels absent.

What happened to chip away at our wholeness? How did disappointments and unmet expectations leave us questioning our worth? Just as a puzzle needs every piece to be complete, our sense of self requires acknowledgment and validation to feel whole—whether in life's big moments or in the simplicity of a meaningful conversation.

PART 1

These early disappointments, though seemingly small, can leave a lasting impact on how we view ourselves, chipping away at our sense of worth and completeness. To illustrate this, let's take Johnny as an example—a five-year-old boy about to face his first experience of unmet expectations. His story reflects how even minor moments can shape our self-perception and begin the cycle of questioning our value.

When Johnny arrived home from his first year of school, he rushed into his dad's office, wide-eyed and full of enthusiasm, "shouting, holding a paper in his hands, "Daddy, daddy, look what I got!" Dad, engrossed in his job in his home office, pays no attention to Johnny.

At this, Johnny shouts even louder, "Daddy, Daddy, look what I got!" Yet, his father's curt response lands like a blow to his fragile heart, as he says, "Johnny! I'm busy! Not now! You have to wait!" Johnny's expectations were shattered when his father's response fell short of the warmth, connection, and approval he had expected.

He is left heartbroken. Johnny's hopes were crushed when his dad's harsh words shattered his expectations. The weight of those hurtful words left him feeling confused, lost, rejected, and not whole. The happy occasion he had imagined, filled with shared laughter and bonding moments, has abruptly transformed into a disheartening reality. That of disappointment!

Let's explore another example.

Meet Mia, whose struggles began at a young age. She was only five years old, living with her father. Despite her age, Mia experienced various challenges that had a lasting impact on her life. During her initial years of schooling, she was known for being playful and joyous.

However, one day, the other children began making fun of her, noticing that she appeared different from the other girls in their class or school. At first, she didn't understand why they were mocking her, but eventually, she realized that she looked different from the other little girls. This realization marked a significant turning point in her life, indicating a shift in her self-perception and how she believed others saw her.

What was different? Mia felt different from other girls because she wore baggy clothes instead of dresses. One day after school, she expressed her desire to wear a dress to her father, but he refused, possibly due to finan cial constraints. How did this make Mia feel? (Remember, she is being made fun of at school for looking different.) This left Mia feeling misunderstood, a sense of not belonging.

To illustrate this further, let's consider Jimmy, a bright and intelligent young boy. Tragically, during his early years, Jimmy's father left his mother and siblings. In time, his mother remarried a man with bullying tendencies who subjected Jimmy to regular physical and verbal abuse. This mistreatment deeply affected Jimmy, leaving lasting scars on his sense of self-worth and trust in others.

One day, the mother discovered that he forced Jimmy to unclog a toilet using his bare hands. Picture this little boy, thrusting his hands as deep as possible into the filthy toilet, removing everything that had come out of it. It's difficult to fathom the emotions Jimmy must have experienced in that moment. Not only was he subjected to verbal abuse, mockery, and scorn, but he was also forced to perform physically dirty tasks.

That lead him to believe that he is not worthy of being heard or understood and therefore concluded "I am unlovable.' What do these three little people, Johnny, Mia and jimmy have in common?

UNWORTHY
OF LOVE AND CARE

Johnny, Mia, and Jimmy were left feeling unworthy of love and care. Each of these children carries a unique story, yet they share a profound commonality: life-altering experiences that left them unable to express their emotions. Without healthy outlets, they suppress their feelings, bottling them up until they manifest in harmful ways. But what does this mean for them—and for us? Their struggles reveal a universal truth: understanding and releasing emotions is essential for fostering healing, self-worth, and growth.

When we're born, we are seen as whole, complete, and perfect beings in the eyes of our caregivers. In those early moments of life, there is no concept of failure, inadequacy, or rejection—just the pure joy of being. We exist in a state of innocence, free from the burdens of judgment or the need for validation. The love and care we receive in those early days reinforce this sense of completeness, making us feel safe and unconditionally accepted.

However, as life unfolds, this natural sense of wholeness begins to face challenges. Disappointments, unmet expectations, and failures—whether large or small—start to chip away at our self-perception. These experiences may seem insignificant at first: a parent's dismissive remark, being excluded by peers, or failing to meet the expectations of others. Yet, over time, their cumulative effect can be profound.

Each moment of rejection, every unmet expectation, or unfulfilled desire begins to shape how we see ourselves. We might start questioning our worth, wondering if we are enough, or if we are deserving of love and care. These doubts settle deep within us, influencing how we navigate the world, how we interact with others, and how we perceive our value.

Though often subtle, these experiences plant seeds of self-doubt that grow into a lens through which we view our lives. They alter the way we relate to ourselves and to others, pulling us further away from the pure, unburdened joy we once knew.

Over time, a sense of incompleteness sets in, as if we're missing a vital piece of our identity. Like a puzzle with gaps, our sense of self becomes fragmented, and we find ourselves searching for validation, acknowledgment, and belonging.

For Johnny, Mia, and Jimmy, this process began early, leaving emotional scars that shaped their self-perception and how they viewed their worth. Johnny's story highlights how an early disappointment can leave a lasting impact.

At five years old, Johnny came home from school excited to show his father an achievement, only to be dismissed with the curt words, "I'm busy! Not now!" In that moment, Johnny's joy and pride turned to confusion and heartbreak, leaving him feeling rejected. Over time, this experience planted a seed of doubt about his worth, making him feel unworthy of love and care.

Mia's challenges began at a young age when she became the target of ridicule at school for not wearing dresses like the other girls. At first, she didn't understand why she was being mocked, but she eventually realized her difference set her apart in a way that felt isolating.

When Mia asked her father for a dress, his refusal left her feeling misunderstood and unsupported. The combination of ridicule at school and her father's unwillingness to address her needs made her feel unworthy of love and care, further deepening her sense of not belonging.

Jimmy's story is perhaps the most heart-wrenching. A bright, intelligent boy, Jimmy faced significant challenges when his father abandoned the family, leaving his mother to remarry a man who was both verbally and physically abusive. This stepfather directed much of his cruelty toward Jimmy, taking advantage of him in degrading ways.

Picture this small boy, forced by his stepfather to unclog a toilet with his bare hands. Thrusting his hands into the filth, he endured not only the physical indignity but also the verbal abuse and scorn that accompanied it. The emotional weight of that moment was overwhelming. Jimmy internalized the belief that he was unworthy of respect or care. He concluded, "If I'm treated this way, I must not be lovable."

These early experiences of rejection, ridicule, and mistreatment left Johnny, Mia, and Jimmy suppressing their emotions and questioning their worth. Each of them, in their own way, internalized the absence of love and care, leading to emotional scars that shaped how they viewed themselves and the world. The inability to express or process these feelings created a pattern of suppression that profoundly impacted their lives. But what happens when emotions are bottled up for too long? Let's explore the repercussions of suppression.

THE REPERCUSSIONS
OF EMOTIONAL NEGECT

Emotions thrive on attentive care and feelings demand timely processing. This means that emotions flourish when they receive attention and acknowledgment, and feelings require to be addressed and processed in a timely manner for a person's well-being.

When emotions are not given the proper care and guidance, they tend to be suppressed rather than processed. This suppression, if left unattended, gradually transforms into a chronic pattern deeply ingrained within the individuals. As time passes, the emotions become increasingly chronically suppressed, leading to lingering feelings that persist until the necessary attention and guidance is provided.

To expand further, let's examine an article featured on CALDA CLINIC's blog on January 24, 2022. The compelling piece, authored by Claudia M. Elsig, MD, delves into the perils associated with suppressing emotions and is aptly titled "The Dangers of Suppressing Emotions."

In addressing the question, 'What does it mean to suppress emotions?' they explain that emotions are natural reactions to what is happening around us, including feelings such as happiness, sadness, and anger. Emotional suppression refers to the act of deliberately or unintentionally pushing away distressing thoughts and feelings from our awareness.

People may use distractions, substance use, overeating, or physical activities to avoid confronting these emotions. If this avoidance becomes a pattern without proper reflection and handling, it can turn into a long-term issue. In children, unprocessed traumatic events or lack of space to express emotions can lead to persistent emotional suppression, allowing feelings to persist despite suppression.

Why do we suppress emotions? There are numerous reasons, such as avoiding socially unacceptable feelings, conforming to societal expectations, and surviving in challenging environments. Emotional suppression is a coping mechanism, allowing us to function effectively in various aspects of life, even though it can lead to anxiety and depression, especially in cases of trauma or abuse.

Suppressing emotions can have both short-term and long-term detrimental effects on the body, manifesting as physiological and psychological issues. Short-term impacts often involve muscle tension, while long-term suppression can lead to anxiety, depression, stress-related illnesses, and potentially substance abuse.

Research has shown that emotional suppression can increase aggression and adversely affect cardiovascular reactivity, with links to mortality observed in various studies. Strong emotions like jealousy, fear, anger, guilt, or remorse, when suppressed, can also have serious consequences, underscoring the importance of acknowledging and processing emotions for overall well-being.

After considering the deep understanding provided in the blog about the long-lasting negative effects of suppressing emotions, think about the significant difficulties that individuals might face due to their emotional suppression. It underscores the gravity of the situation for these individuals and the obstacles they may encounter as a result of their emotional struggles.

This brings to mind an essential truth I heard while watching a TV show, where a character said something that stuck with me: 'the past affects the future.' It means that what happened before can shape what comes later. Think about the big challenges Johnny, Mia, and Jimmy face as they navigate the impact of their past experiences.

Their life experiences, much like any others we may encounter, possess the capacity to cause changing consequences that can reverberate throughout our future and overall well-being. Whether it is the sting of rejection, the anguish of abuse, or the mere disappointment of a resounding "no," such events have the power to etch indelible imprints upon our psychological and emotional development.

These formative encounters have the potential to shape the very core of our beliefs, influence our behavioral patterns, and profoundly impact the dynamics of our relationships as we traverse the intricate tapestry of life.

In the struggles to make sense of these challenging experiences, especially at a young age, children often come to erroneous conclusions—forming assumptions, opinions, or perceptions of themselves, the world, or life that may not be true. They might believe they are unworthy of love, that the world is a harsh place, or that life is filled only with disappointment.

Such beliefs, rooted in past experiences, can deeply influence the way they see themselves and how they engage with the world.

For example, Johnny's intentions and expectations were shattered when his father overlooked, disregarded, and dismissed him, leaving him with a deep sense of invalidation.

Along with feelings of anger, disappointment, sadness, and embarrassment, the experience was profoundly disheartening, making him feel unacknowledged and unappreciated. Despite his tender age and limited ability to express his emotions verbally, Johnny internalized two powerful beliefs: 'I am not important, and my existence holds no value.'

In response, he made a firm decision: 'I will never, ever, do the thing that got me in trouble, and I won't share my accomplishments with anyone.'

These conclusions shaped his view of himself and the world, as he equated sharing with the risk of rejection and emotional pain.

Similarly, Mia has been deprived of the ability to make choices for herself, ridiculed, and dismissed by her father. She is made to feel that her requests are insignificant, leaving her feeling unheard, misunderstood, and questioning her own worth and validity. As a result, Mia forms the belief that her needs and voice don't matter, and that she is powerless. This belief will become ingrained in her memory, shaping how she responds to future situations where she feels disregarded or unimportant.

Likewise, Jimmy faced a different kind of trauma in his early years. After his father left, his mother remarried a man with bullying tendencies. This stepfather subjected Jimmy to both physical and verbal abuse, including a particularly degrading incident where Jimmy was forced to unclog a toilet with his bare hands.

This experience left Jimmy emotionally scarred, eroding his self-esteem and making it difficult for him to cultivate a healthy sense of self-worth.

As a result, Jimmy came to believe that he was worthless and powerless, constantly at the mercy of others' cruelty. This belief, ingrained in his memory, will shape his reactions in future situations where he feels humiliated or controlled.

Based on the experiences of Mia, Jimmy, and Johnny, it becomes clear how early impactful events can shape the core beliefs we hold about ourselves and the world. These beliefs, whether accurate or distorted, influence how we navigate future challenges and define our sense of worth and identity.

But what, exactly, is a belief? Where do these convictions come from, and how do they take root in our minds? Let's delve into the next chapter to explore these questions and uncover the powerful role beliefs play in shaping our lives.

CHAPTER TWO:

WHAT IS BELIEF?

According to the Stanford Encyclopedia of Philosophy, contemporary Anglophone philosophers of mind commonly employ the term "belief" to denote the attitude we possess when we consider something to be true or regard it as the case. Other sources define a belief as a perception of reality.

The Oxford dictionary defines it this way: a way of regarding, understanding, or interpreting something; a mental impression. So, a belief can be described as a manner of perceiving or interpreting something—an impression formed within the mind.

The guest house puts it this way: We hold three core types of beliefs. Within each of those core types of beliefs are many different subtypes of beliefs. First, we hold beliefs about ourselves. Second, we hold beliefs about others.

Lastly, we hold beliefs about the world around us. Our beliefs in each of these areas shape our perceptions and perspectives which ultimately shape our reality.

When we examine our beliefs, identify them, articulate them, and discover their origin, we are empowered to decide our reality. MMA fighter TJ Dillashaw stated "Belief is a powerful thing".

Beliefs are so powerful that they can shape how we feel about ourselves, others, and the world around us. Once we realize that our beliefs shape our reality and our beliefs can be changed, we start to change the reality of our lives.

So, a belief is a perception, a way of regarding, understanding, or interpreting something. It is an interpretation of how something or how life occurs to us. Beliefs can be pretty powerful.

They are the driving force of your actions; they drive you to do things without you realizing it. They form without you being aware of it. Especially when you are young and still figuring out how to navigate life, your perception of events can become deeply rooted.

In the way of storytelling, you can uncover the views you formed long ago and strongly believed in, which now influence how you see things. These stories, akin to narratives in our minds, shape our thought patterns.

By taking the time to reflect on these stories, we can unravel their origins and identify other specific beliefs that have stemmed from them.

Below is a compilation of beliefs that may restrict your success, happiness, and freedom. Please identify and circle the ones that apply to you or the ones you believe hinder and constrain you in your pursuits.

- I can't achieve my goals.
- I will never succeed.
- I always make mistakes.
- I can't trust anyone.
- I don't have enough time to improve my life.
- I feel awkward in social situations.
- The world feels cold and uncaring.
- I don't know what I truly want in life.
- I'm broken or flawed.
- I need to please others to avoid rejection.
- I have to stay in a toxic relationship because I can't make it on my own.
- I am unattractive, guilty, and afraid.
- Success requires constant struggle.
- I will never change for the better.

- I am alone and insignificant.
- I'm not worthy of success.
- I'll never have enough resources.
- I am helpless and inferior to others.
- I'm boring and uninteresting.
- I am unworthy of love.
- If I express myself, I'll be judged or rejected.
- I am powerless to control my life.
- I am not special or unique.
- I am ineffective and incapable.
- I am incomplete.
- I am slow, unintelligent, and unworthy.
- I am not valuable to anyone.
- My existence doesn't matter.
- If something hasn't happened yet, it never will.
- I am inadequate in every way.
- I don't deserve happiness or care.
- I am unacceptable to others.
- If people loved me, they'd prove it differently.
- My efforts will always fail.
- I am too old to start over.
- I am unfit for success or belonging.
- I need to control everything to feel secure.
- There's something fundamentally wrong with me.
- Life is too hard for me to handle.
- I can't stand up for myself.
- I can't set boundaries or say no.
- My happiness depends on others, not me.
- I don't belong anywhere.
- Only the rich thrive; I'm stuck in poverty.
- I don't deserve love or care.
- Time is always against me.
- People take advantage of me, and I can't stop it.
- The world is unsafe and full of threats.
- I am unhealthy and destined to fail.
- No matter what I do, it's never enough.
- Mistakes define me and make me unworthy.
- I am nothing and have no purpose.
- I am always a second choice.

If you can think of any other beliefs that we may have missed in this list, which could be contributing to what is limiting you in your endeavors, please write them down below.

_____

_____

_____

_____

_____

THE POWER
OF EARLY EXPERIENCES

Based on the experiences of Mia, Jimmy, and Johnny, it becomes clear how early impactful events can shape the core beliefs we hold about ourselves and the world. These beliefs, whether accurate or distorted, influence how we navigate future challenges and define our sense of worth and identity.

How exactly do beliefs start, and why do they come to hold such power over us?

A belief is often formed when someone experiences a significant, emotionally charged incident and tries to make sense of it. In that moment, the mind seeks to understand what happened by forming opinions and assumptions.

These initial thoughts, often based on confusion or shock, can solidify into a belief if they aren't questioned.

When Lucy experienced an inappropriate incident with her uncle, she froze, unable to process what was happening. In her confusion, she tried to make sense of the event, forming assumptions like, "there is something wrong here?" or "Is this my fault?" These unchallenged thoughts solidified into a belief about herself: "There's something wrong with me."

This belief, rooted in shame and self-doubt, became the foundation for how she saw herself and affected her interactions with others. Over time, it influenced her behavior, decisions, and emotional responses, reinforcing a cycle of uncertainty and fear.

Storytelling has a unique power to unravel the layers of deeply held beliefs, gradually exposing their origins. Lucy's story will illustrate this process, showing how life's experiences shape our perceptions. As she recounts her journey, we see how moments of confusion, disappointment, and discomfort lay the foundation for the beliefs she forms about herself.

Through Lucy's narrative, we deconstruct how beliefs take shape—often unconsciously—and subtly influence the decisions we make. By examining her story, we reveal how these beliefs become intertwined with her sense of identity, demonstrating how storytelling can illuminate and transform the hidden assumptions that shape our lives.

PART 2

2

UNCOVERING THE ROOTS

CHAPTER THREE:
THE LUCY STORY

Lucy's story centers on a beautiful young girl named Lucy. Her captivating beauty earns her the affectionate nickname "La Bonita" (The Pretty One) from her loving father, uncles, and aunts. With her striking appearance, quiet demeanor, and obedient nature, she quickly becomes the cherished focus of attention in her village.

Her father, in particular, holds her dear, consistently showing his affection through his words and actions. After long, grueling days of work in the fields, his first act upon returning home is to call out her name with warmth and joy, "Lucy, Lucy!"

Now, let Lucy guide us through her story. She will take us by the hand, leading us through the defining moments and intricate details of her life. From her perspective, we will gain valuable insights and witness the events that shaped her journey.

Lucy:
The village, and especially my father, lovingly called me "La Bonita," the pretty one—a name that filled me with joy and a deep sense of being loved.

My father's affection for me was evident in the way he always brought me the finest fruits from the fields, handpicked with care.

Those simple but meaningful gestures made me feel treasured and valued beyond measure. I basked in the warmth of being his favorite, feeling like the centerpiece of everyone's affection.

It wasn't just my father who lavished me with love. My older siblings joined in, offering me gifts, kind words, and tender embraces. Even neighbors and visitors from other towns seemed drawn to me.

I remember a particular family from a nearby town who, enchanted by my presence, asked my mother if they could take me with them for a while. To my surprise, my mother agreed without hesitation, reinforcing my belief that I was truly special and adored by all. At that time, I didn't yet understand concepts like good or bad—life simply was. My existence felt harmonious and whole, untouched by complexity.

But then, an event occurred that shattered my sense of innocence and altered the rhythm of my life forever. One day, everything changed. The peace and simplicity I had known were replaced by confusion and unease. The world, once so vibrant and full of love, began to reveal its darker corners, and I found myself struggling to comprehend this new reality. The sharp clarity of right and wrong, joy and trust, blurred into uncertainty, leaving me disoriented and longing for the purity of my earlier days.

That moment became a turning point in my life. It marked the end of my untainted innocence and the beginning of a journey that would redefine my understanding of the world and myself.

Standing at the threshold of this unfamiliar territory, I realized that this event, as painful and confusing as it was, would shape the course of my life in profound and lasting ways.

What was the defining moment that so deeply changed Lucy's outlook on life? How did a single event shift everything for her? Let's hear from her as she continues.

PART 2

SITUATION NO. 1

THE TURNING POINT:
THE MOMENT OF FRACTURE

Lucy:

One quiet Sunday afternoon, I was happily playing under the shade of a tree, enjoying the simple joys of childhood. A soft breeze drifted by, and suddenly, I heard a familiar voice calling my name, "Lucy, Lucy!"

Curious, I turned toward the sound and stood up.
The voice continued with an urgent plea, "Lucy, Lucy! Come here!"
Drawn by my obedient nature, I walked toward the voice without hesitation. As I passed by a bedroom, I saw my uncle reclining on a cot, looking up at me. He called out again, this time more urgently, "Lucy! It's me. I need your help. Please, get my cigarettes—they're on top of the dresser."

His tone seemed earnest, so I stepped closer and reached for the pack of cigarettes. But as I handed them to him, something happened that left me feeling deeply unsettled. His actions made me uncomfortable, leaving me with a peculiar sensation I didn't understand.

A strange, unfamiliar feeling washed over me, leaving me frozen and uneasy. My young mind swirled with confusion, trying to make sense of the moment. "What is this feeling?" I wondered silently, unable to fully process what had just happened. Deep within me, a voice whispered, like an alarm trying to protect me: "This is wrong."

Even in my innocence, I could feel something wasn't right. Though I couldn't fully understand or articulate it, a deep discomfort welled up inside me. It was as if my very instincts were warning me that a line had been crossed, even if I didn't yet understand the concept of boundaries or consent.

I felt stuck—confused and overwhelmed, unable to move or speak. A heavy sense of shame crept in, as if I were somehow to blame for something I didn't even comprehend. My inner voice tried to guide me, but I was too young to know how to act on it.

Lucy felt an oppressive discomfort settle over her, leaving her paralyzed and unable to grasp what had just unfolded.

A heavy silence seemed to steal her voice as she stood frozen, stuck in a moment where time felt suspended, her confusion and uncertainty overwhelming her ability to act or understand.

THE FREEZE RESPONSE: WHEN SHAME AND CONFUSION TAKE HOLD

In the book "Rewire Your Anxious Brain" by Catherine M. Pittman and Elizabeth M. Karle, it is explained that humans have three common responses when faced with challenging situations. These responses are often referred to as fight, flight, or freeze, similar to how a deer freezes when caught in the glare of headlights.

The article titled "Understanding the Freeze Response" by Hanan Parvez, published on May 9, 2021, explains how the freeze response functions. Parvez said:

"Many believe that our first reaction to stress or impending danger is the fight-or-flight response. But before we take flight or fight, we need some time to assess the situation and decide what the best course of action would be- to fight or to run away. This results in what is known as 'the freeze response' and is experienced when we face a stressful or fearful situation. The freeze response has a couple of easily identifiable physical symptoms. The body becomes still as if we've been riveted (fixed, rooted) to the spot. Breathing becomes shallow, to the point that one may hold their breath for some time. The duration of this freeze response may range from a few milliseconds to a few seconds, depending on the gravity of the situation. Sometimes, after freezing, we may not be able to decide between fight and flight but continue in our frozen state because this is the best that we can do to ensure our survival. In other words, we freeze to just freeze. This is an example of disassociation. The experience is so traumatic and dreadful, the mind, like the body, just switches off."

At times, when faced with a difficult situation, we might find ourselves unable to choose between fighting or running away. Instead, we remain frozen, as if it's the only way to keep ourselves safe. It's like we freeze just to freeze. This is known as dissociation. The experience is so overwhelmingly distressing that our mind, much like our body, simply shuts down. This is the case with Lucy.

The unsettling incident leaves an indelible mark on Lucy, shifting her perception of herself, others, and the world. Though she cannot recall how she left her uncle's presence, the experience begins to shape her beliefs, emotions, and interactions. This pivotal moment sets the stage for a journey filled with challenges and complexities that will influence her thoughts and attitudes moving forward. Lucy later reflected on the experience, expressing it in her own words.

Lucy:

In that moment, my mind fills with so many thoughts and feelings. Shame washes over me, and I freeze, stuck in my own embarrassment. I want to leave, but I can't move. It feels like my whole world has fallen apart. I just wish I could disappear, like the ground would open up and swallow me. I don't want anyone to see me; I want to be invisible, like I was never here.

Lucy feels an overwhelming sense of loss, as though her dignity has been stripped away, leaving her exposed and vulnerable. This traumatic event causes her to disconnect from her sense of self, leaving her numb and detached—not just from the world around her, but from her very essence.

According to "The Science of Emotion: Exploring the Basics of Emotional Psychology" article, which was posted on June 27, 2019, by UWA | Psychology and Counseling News, our interpretation and response to events shape our identity and affect our well-being. For someone as young as Lucy, who may not yet have the words to explain what just happened, this concept takes on even greater significance.

You see, at a young age, children are still learning to express themselves. Just as babies initially communicate through sensations and emotions, young children also respond to the world around them in ways that are not fully verbal.

Without the cognitive and linguistic skills needed to articulate complex feelings, children like Lucy often rely on their instincts and emotional reactions to make sense of confusing experiences.

Studies show that while young children may be aware of what they feel, they often lack the vocabulary to explain these sensations. This reliance on emotions as a primary mode of communication shapes their developing sense of self and the way they navigate difficult situations.

So, thoughts and perceptions enter their young minds through the medium of touch, physical sensations, and emotional responses. They might feel the warmth or coldness of their surroundings, experience comfort or discomfort in certain situations, and respond accordingly.

However, since their cognitive faculties are not fully developed, they often lack the vocabulary necessary to express themselves adequately.

Furthermore, the capacity to distinguish between right and wrong, particularly in the context of distressing or disturbing events, is still in the early stages of development. This lack of cognitive maturity and linguistic proficiency hinders their ability to comprehend and articulate their experiences in a comprehensive manner.

As a result, young children often suppress their emotions and thoughts, inadvertently bottling them up without even realizing it. This internalized suppression occurs due to their limited understanding and the absence of suitable means to convey their distress.

The complex nature of their emotions and the inability to express them verbally lead to an unintentional suppression that young children are not conscious of.

Given Lucy's young age and limited linguistic abilities, it poses a challenge for her to communicate the violation of her dignity effectively. In such a situation, she may resort to alternative means of expression, primarily through non-verbal cues and behavioral changes.

These could manifest as changes in her mood, temperament, or overall demeanor. She may display signs of distress, such as increased agitation, withdrawal, or changes in her usual patterns of behavior.

Additionally, Lucy might exhibit physical reactions like crying, clinging to familiar individuals, or avoiding certain situations or people associated with the incident.

It is crucial for caregivers and professionals to be attentive to these non-verbal signals and provide a supportive and safe environment that encourages children to express their emotions in a way that feels comfortable for them.

Lucy's story shows us how early, overwhelming emotions—like

shame and embarrassment—can leave a lasting impact, particularly when they are left unaddressed. Without guidance or reassurance, Lucy is left alone with her feelings, leading her to construct her own interpretations of what happened.

These interpretations become the foundation of her beliefs, influencing her sense of self and the way she interacts with the world.

In the next chapter, we'll explore how young minds process difficult emotions and form beliefs about themselves and others.

By examining Lucy's experience, we gain insight into how our own early encounters can shape the beliefs that guide us, often unconsciously, throughout our lives.

PART 2

CHAPTER FOUR:
INSIDE THE EMOTIONAL RESPONSE

Regrettably, Lucy was left to cope with her feelings of shame and embarrassment without proper support or guidance. With no one to tell her that the incident was not her fault and that it was morally wrong.

The American Psychological Association (APA), defines emotion as "a complex reaction pattern, involving experiential, behavioral and physiological elements." Emotions are how individuals deal with matters or situations they find personally significant.

Emotional experiences have three components:
a subjective experience, a physiological response, and a behavioral or expressive response. Said in simple words, The American Psychological Association (APA) explains that emotions are complex reactions we have when something significant happens to us.

They involve how we feel, how our body responds, and how we act. When we experience emotions, three things happen: we have a personal and unique feeling inside us, our body reacts in certain ways, and we show our emotions through our behavior and actions.

What is the subjective experience, reaction or what is Lucy's personal and unique perception, interpretation, and emotional response to this particular situation or event?

In other words what is her internal and subjective aspect of her experience which includes her feelings, thoughts, and emotional state. Since the subjective experience refers to the specific and personal feeling she went through. It could be a mix of emotions such as shame, embarrassment, or discomfort.

This unique feeling is her own individual emotional response to the situation she faced, which are specific to her and her individual reaction to the situation. This subjective experience is shaped by her own thoughts, feelings, and interpretations of the event, and it may differ from how others perceive or react to the same incident.

What is the physiological response, or the body responses? Physiological response refers to the body's automatic reactions and changes that occur in response to various stimuli, such as emotional or stressful situations. These responses can include physical sensations, changes in heart rate, blood pressure, breathing patterns, hormonal releases, and other bodily functions.

Lucy said she felt as if everything in her world had fallen apart, the desire to vanish consumes her, and hoped for the ground to split open and devour her whole. This suggests intense emotional distress. The physiological response to such distress might manifest as an increased heart rate, shallow breathing, sweaty palms, or other bodily sensations associated with anxiety or stress.

She said, in her mind, "I want to hide," this need to hide and the thought of not wanting anyone to see her shows a heightened sense of self-awareness and the physiological response of heightened vigilance.

When someone feels the need to hide or avoid being seen by others, it often indicates that they are conscious of their presence and how they might be perceived by others. This self- awareness can arise from a heightened sensitivity to their emotional state or a concern about being judged or exposed. It suggests that they are acutely attuned to their surroundings and the potential reactions of others.

Overall, the need to hide and the reluctance to be seen reflect both an

increased self- awareness and a physiological response of heightened vigilance, indicating the individual's heightened sensitivity and alertness to their surroundings and the people around them.

So, in Lucy's case, the psychological response or body response refers to the reactions occurring within her mind and body as a result of the incident. These responses manifested as physical sensations, changes in heart rate, breathing patterns, muscle tension, and other physiological reactions.

What is the behavior or expressive response? Behavioral response refers to the observable actions, reactions, or behaviors that an individual displays in response to a particular situation, stimulus, or event. It encompasses the outward expressions, gestures, verbalizations, or physical actions that can be observed and measured by others.

According to experts, in the context of human behavior, a behavioral response can be influenced by various factors such as emotions, thoughts, beliefs, and environmental cues. It represents how an individual chooses to act or behave based on their internal processes and external circumstances.

So, what was Lucy's behavior or expressive response? Or how did she demonstrate her emotions outwardly through her actions and behaviors? As it is common for individuals to exhibit various behaviors when expressing their emotions.

These behaviors could include crying, withdrawing from others, avoiding certain situations or individuals associated with the incident, displaying signs of distress or agitation, or seeking comfort and support from trusted individuals. This is exactly how Lucy responded as her behavioral response.

In order to protect herself from re-experiencing the pain, she actively avoided situations or things that could trigger or remind her of the traumatic experiences. This included staying away from specific places, people, activities, and discussions that could bring back painful memories or emotions. That was definitely a 'what just happened' moment for her.

TRIGGERS &
SELF PERCEPTIONS

The American Psychological Association (APA) article also highlights those emotions, like everything else, have a starting point. Therefore, it raises the question: What is the initial trigger that leads to Lucy's feelings of shame and embarrassment?

Dr. Joe Dispenza, another one of my mentors explained what happens in our brain when in the midst of an experience— he said, "when we are in the midst of an experience, all of our five senses plug us into the external environment (your antennas to the outer world).

As your brain is processing all this vital sensory data, all this information is rushing back to the brain. When it reaches the brain, it causes jungles of neurons to organize themselves into networks (a group or system of interconnections to interact with one another to exchange information).

These networks string into patterns to reflect the interaction with the external environment. The moment those neurons organize into patterns the brain makes a chemical. That chemical is an emotion.

So here you are, in the midst of an experience, and what happens next? As Lucy finds herself engaged with the external environment, her senses begin collecting data to send to her brain.

In this case, the sensation of touch triggers a reaction within her body, evoking a feeling of disgust. This sensory information is transmitted to her brain, where networks of neurons begin organizing into specific patterns that mirror her experience. At the moment these neurons connect, the brain generates a chemical reaction—a corresponding emotion.

In Lucy's case, this emotion is shame, formed almost instantaneously. Since the brain processes experiences through mental imagery, the picture Lucy holds in her mind is imbued with feelings of both shame and disgust.

Lucy's starting point is when she freezes. In the moment she senses the inappropriate touch, it alarms her as something unfamiliar and wrong. Contextualize it, she interprets the event in her own way.

Based on her perception and interpretation, she creates a story about herself.

In that exact moment, Lucy's young mind and body register feelings of shame and embarrassment. In a split second, she thinks, 'I am embarrassed.' She feels this way because she perceives the incident as something unclean, leading to a belief expressed through her feelings: 'I am unclean.'

From this, she reasons, 'If I am unclean, then I am worthless and unwanted.'

This interpretation takes hold, and she begins to feel dirty, worthless, and unwanted, believing she has been tainted and rendered impure.

Although this publication is not specifically about sexual abuse, the following note is for readers who have experienced this kind of trauma:

When such an unfamiliar experience occurs, a child might have the following thoughts:

• Confusion: The child may feel unsure why they are being touched inappropriately, particularly if they lack understanding of the situation or have not been taught about personal boundaries.

• Fear: They might experience fear due to the violation of their personal space and the discomfort caused by the inappropriate touch. This fear could extend to the person involved or the potential consequences of speaking up.

• Guilt or self-blame: Children may mistakenly believe they are to blame, feeling that they did something wrong to deserve the behavior or that they are somehow responsible.

• Shame or embarrassment: They may feel a sense of shame or embarrassment due to the invasion of their privacy and the inappropriate nature of the touch. They might also worry about being judged if others find out.

• Anger or frustration: older children, in particular, may feel anger or frustration toward the person who violated their boundaries, recognizing the harm and injustice caused.

Understanding these reactions can help foster compassion and provide insight into the emotional impact such experiences can have on a child.

If we have suffered a similar experience, we may feel unsure of ourselves, needing reassurance and comfort.

When that does not happen, feelings of embarrassment, shame, and diminished self-worth can take hold. Lucy, as a little girl, does not fully understand these emotions but instinctively suppresses them, pushing them down internally. Over time, without awareness, these unresolved feelings shape attitudes, behaviors, and beliefs that affect her life.

As a result, Lucy's behavior begins to change. Her once joyful and free demeanor is replaced by visible signs of withdrawal. Her posture becomes hunched, her face tilts downward, and her hair seems to act as a shield from the world.

It's as if she's silently saying, "Please don't look at me; I feel exposed!" She avoids eye contact, hesitates to respond when spoken to, and begins to question her worth. Lucy starts to wonder if she is still acceptable, loved, or wanted.

THE IMPACT
OF ALTERED THOUGHTS

Lucy's life takes a dramatic turn as her actions begin to align with her new self- perception. Although these changes originate as thoughts, her emotional engagement with them gives them power.

Bob Proctor, a renowned self-help author, explains that deeply engaging with a thought over time ignites a powerful catalyst, shaping actions and outcomes. The self-image Lucy now holds—rooted in her subconscious—governs her behavior, decisions, and demeanor.

Neuroscientists explain that thoughts arise from complex neural interactions in the brain. These neural networks process information through electrical impulses, forming patterns that shape how we think, feel, and perceive the world. This connection between thoughts and emotions demonstrates how Lucy's beliefs now directly influence her actions and outlook on life.

Lucy once radiated joy and empathy, embracing the world with curiosity and enthusiasm. Her presence brought peace and comfort to others, but this radiance has dimmed.

She now sees herself through a lens of self-doubt and insecurity, distorting her perception of others and the world around her.

What once felt vibrant and full of possibility is now overshadowed by skepticism and mistrust.

Lucy's distorted self-image leads her to project her insecurities onto others, making trust and connection difficult. She believes others see her flaws just as she does, creating a cycle of self-criticism and isolation. This mindset deepens her feelings of unworthiness and limits her ability to appreciate the beauty in herself and others.

As life unfolds, new experiences create additional beliefs that build on existing perceptions. In the next chapter, we'll explore how Lucy's core beliefs evolve into a web of related thoughts, shaping her identity and actions in profound ways.

PART 2

CHAPTER FIVE:

HIDDEN ROOTS: THE WEIGHT OF UNSPOKEN BELIEFS

This chapter looks at how our beliefs evolve and branch out over time, much like a growing tree. Our core beliefs act as roots, anchoring us and shaping our perspective on the world.

As we experience life, these roots give rise to new beliefs—branches that extend from the foundation we've built. Each branch represents an additional belief connected to the core, forming a complex network that guides our thoughts and actions.

Our first experience with negativity can shape how we see ourselves and affect our entire lives. For Lucy, believing 'I am broken' made her think others saw her that way too, which changed how she felt about herself and how she acted around others.

As Lucy's story goes on, we see how negative thoughts took over her mind, telling her, 'I am dirty, worthless, and unwanted.' She took these thoughts to heart and began to believe she was beyond help. This belief led her to withdraw and stop speaking, as if her voice had been taken away. She stayed silent, thinking no one wanted to hear her, because she felt tainted and broken inside. Lucy's silence became a symbol of how deeply that early negative experience affected her. She believed that others saw her as she saw herself, which made her retreat even more. She carried herself with a slouched posture, avoided eye contact, and kept to herself. This way of thinking influenced her actions, which then affected how people around her responded.

In short, our core beliefs can shape how we act, and those actions influence how others respond to us. Lucy thought she was tainted, so she withdrew, assuming no one would want to be near her.

Her body language and silence reflected how she felt inside, showing how powerful our beliefs can be in shaping our reality.

HOW CORE BELIEFS DRIVE OUR ACTIONS AND SHAPE OTHER'S REACTIONS

Convinced that she was 'tainted and unwanted,' Lucy's demeanor shifted, leading to noticeable changes in her behavior. Yet, unaware of her traumatic encounter, those around her misinterpreted her silence as something odd or amusing, responding with mockery rather than compassion.

Her withdrawn behavior became a target for ridicule, as siblings, aunts, uncles, and neighbors repeatedly taunted her, saying, "she doesn't talk, the cat got her tongue."

She heard that phrase so often that, over time, she stopped speaking altogether. Even when she tried, the persistent ridicule caused her to stutter. To her young mind, those words became a painful truth as she reasoned, "If I can't express my thoughts, I must be dumb."

These beliefs—that she is broken, unwanted, and unable to express herself—begin to shape her sense of self, causing her to struggle with communication, often appearing withdrawn and at a loss for words.

Stuttering when speaking leads to embarrassment and deepens her discomfort, creating a cycle where her negative beliefs seem to take shape in her reality.

This cycle aligns with the Law of Attraction, which suggests that the thoughts we focus on—whether positive or negative—bring corresponding experiences into our lives.

According to this popular theory, positive thoughts bring positive results, whereas negative thoughts bring negative outcomes. While some believe in its power, others remain skeptical.

Yet, regardless of our stance, there is a simple truth: what we focus our energy on tends to come back to us.

Lucy, however, focuses not on the beautiful little girl she truly is, but on the hurtful beliefs she holds about herself—that she is dirty, worthless, dumb, and unwanted.

As a result, she retreats into herself. She walks hunched over, hides her face behind her hair, and avoids looking others in the eye. Now, she actively searches for evidence to support these beliefs, and in doing so, she is likely to find exactly what she's expecting. Let's see how this unfolds.

SITUATION NO. 2

THE FIRST SEEDS
OF FEELING UNWANTED

When Lucy was 8 years old, her peaceful nap was interrupted by a distressing dream. She woke up engulfed in fear, confusion, and loneliness, prompting her to seek her mother's comfort.

Tearfully, she approached her mother, who was busy washing dishes in the kitchen. As Lucy clung to her mother's apron, desperate for attention, her mother turned to her with visible annoyance and snapped, "Stop crying, you crybaby. Can't you see I'm busy?"

Startled and heartbroken, Lucy's tears abruptly stopped. She had sought love and understanding but was met with rejection. Her mother's dismissive response deeply wounded her, and she walked back to her room, feeling dejected and alone.

Later, when she woke again, the lingering sadness and disappointment deterred her from approaching her mother a second time. In her young mind, Lucy came to a profound realization: adults were unavailable for comfort or support, and she must face her emotions alone.

This belief—that she was alone and could not rely on others—became a cornerstone of Lucy's growing self-perception. It was further reinforced by the idea that seeking attention made her a burden.

Her mother's harsh words, "Get away from me, you crybaby," echoed in her mind, cementing the thought: "I am bothering people."

With this conclusion, Lucy resolved to navigate her emotions and challenges independently, convinced that seeking help was futile.

As Lucy's belief system expanded, the thought "I am alone and on my own" became a driving force in her life. It shaped her behavior, discouraging her from reaching out for support and compelling her to shoulder burdens alone.

This pattern of self-reliance grew stronger over time, laying the foundation for how Lucy interacted with others and approached life's challenges.

SITUATION NO. 3

THE GROWING
NETWORK OF SELF-PERCEPTION

One night, Lucy is startled awake by her father's urgent voice calling her name. Confused, she sits up and asks, "Why are you waking me up?" Her father, sounding frightened, replies, "Get up! Go get your sister. Your mom is very sick and might be dying."

Lucy's heart pounds. She had known her mother was unwell but had never considered losing her.

Overwhelmed with panic, she quickly puts on her shoes and runs five blocks to her sister's house. Bursting in, she shouts, "Lina, wake up! Dad says Mom is dying!"

Lina, still groggy, gets up and follows Lucy back to their parents' house.

When they arrive, Lucy sees a group of people gathered around her mother. Instead of going inside, Lucy stays in the courtyard under the moon-light, a deep sense of confusion and dread settling in her chest.

In that moment, overwhelmed by the thought of losing her mother, Lucy presses her hands to her heart and whispers silently, "If this is the pain of losing someone you love, I vow to never, ever love again."

These words carve themselves into her mind and heart, shaping her belief system. A profound emotional numbness envelops her as if a part of her has died. She begins to associate love with unbearable pain and decides she must shut herself off from love to avoid further suffering.

From that day forward, Lucy starts to emotionally disconnect—not only from her mother but from everyone she loves. Her belief that loves leads to devastating pain becomes deeply ingrained, and she gradually isolates her-self from others. She becomes a loner—not lonely, but distant and detached.

Her emotions grow cold, and she withdraws into herself, thinking, "I am alone and on my own."

Though Lucy's mother survives, the emotional impact of that night shapes her deeply. She carries her decision to shield herself from love into ev-ery relationship, her detachment and guardedness becoming a defining part of her personality. As we grow into adulthood, our minds become crowded with a myriad of beliefs about life.

These beliefs form the foundation of our personal narratives, ex-plaining why we perceive certain limitations or obstacles, why we doubt our capabilities, and why we hesitate to pursue progress. This "I can't" mentality, along with self-doubt and justifications for inaction, shapes how we approach life's challenges and opportunities. Over time, these negative beliefs can accu-mulate, influencing not only our perceptions but also our potential.

Our belief system functions like a tree, with a core belief as its trunk. From this central belief, additional beliefs branch out as we encounter new experiences.

These branches, representing different aspects of our lives, evolve as we interpret and respond to the world around us. Each new experience adds another layer, shaping our perspective and reinforcing or challenging our existing beliefs.

As Lucy grows, her life becomes intertwined with a narrative shaped by her beliefs, perspectives, and perceptions. She begins to live within the story she has created about herself—a story that dictates how she sees life, interprets her worth, and imagines how others view her. Her actions, decisions, and interactions are guided by this self-constructed narrative, reflecting the profound influence of her beliefs on her identity and choices.

———IN SUMMARY FROM INCIDENT 1———

Our core beliefs shape our actions, which in turn influence how others respond to us. This applies to Lucy, who believes she is defiled and keeps it a secret by staying silent. She thinks nobody would want to be around her, making her feel unwanted, worthless, and unlovable. Thus, Lucy behaves in a certain way and has a particular demeanor.

She carries herself with a hunched posture, avoids eye contact, and remains silent when approached by others. People around her, unaware of her experience, mock her and make fun of her silence, calling her "dumb" and saying 'the cat got her tongue.'

Hearing these phrases repeatedly, Lucy believes she can't express herself properly and gradually stops speaking. The constant reminder of being called "dumb" makes her stutter. This reinforces her belief that she is unintelligent.

Due to this new belief, she may appear withdrawn, struggle to communicate, and experience difficulty engaging in conversations. Unaware of the underlying belief shaping her actions, Lucy reacts with confusion and continues to stutter.

This reinforces her self-consciousness, and she encounters more situations that intensify her embarrassment, aligning with the concept of the 'law of attraction.'

———IN SUMMARY FROM INCIDENT 2———

During a nap at 8 years old, Lucy had a distressing dream that left her feeling fearful, confused, and lonely. Upon waking up she sought her mother's comfort but was met with dismissive and harsh responses. This shattered her heart and led her to believe that adults were inaccessible and an unreliable for support.

This belief was internalized and became deeply ingrained. Convinced that reaching out to others would be in vain, she refrained from seeking help from people, but expecially from adults. The belief became stronger when her mother's dismissive response reinforced it. From that moment on, Lucy firmly believed that she was alone and on her own. This shaped her behavior and fueled her determination to face life's obstacles independently.

———IN SUMMARY FROM INCIDENT 3———

Lucy is abruptly awakened in the middle of the night by her father, who urgently informs her that her mother is in critical condition and dying.

This shocking news overwhelms her, and she rushes to get her sister before returning to their parents' house. Standing outside, Lucy experiences a deep emotional pain and decides to never love again, believing that the pain of losing someone is unbearable.

This decision shapes her perspective on relationships and love, leading her to disconnect from her emotions and become distant and uncaring. She isolates herself and becomes emotionally numb, like a cold rock, detaching from the world and everyone in it.

FROM
SUPPRESSION TO EXPRESSION

Many of us struggle to process and understand our emotions, often because we didn't have the tools or support to develop these skills. As a result, we suppress our feelings, unaware of the long-term impact on our well-being.

If you've ever felt unable to express your emotions or faced disappointment, rejection, or ridicule, writing can be a powerful tool for self-reflection and healing. Start by writing about a time you felt disappointed, describing how it affected you personally.

Consider these prompts as you reflect on your experiences: Have you ever felt...

PART 2

- Rejected
- Ignored
- Judged
- Humiliated
- Belittled
- Deprived
- Mocked
- Devalued
- Demoralized
- Shamed
- Bullied

Once you've identified a specific experience, ask yourself:

1. What emotion did I feel in that moment?

_____
_____
_____
_____

2. What belief arose from this experience?

_____
_____
_____
_____

3. How did this belief shape my behavior?

_____
_____
_____

4. How did it affect my demeanor or attitude?

_____
_____
_____
_____

5. What narrative or story have I created around this belief?

_____
_____
_____
_____

Lucy's story exemplifies how suppressed emotions and beliefs shape our lives.

PART 2

• Emotions and struggles: Lucy carries shame, fear, anger, loneliness, and anxiety. These heavy emotions significantly impact her mental and emotional well-being.

• Core beliefs: She believes she is tainted, unworthy, unclean, and unwanted. These beliefs dominate her thoughts and skew her self-perception.

• Behavioral impact: Lucy's demeanor reflects her inner struggles—she walks with a hunched posture, avoids eye contact, shields her face with her hair, struggles to communicate effectively and her voice seems silenced, overshadowed by her shame.

• Pervasive influence: These beliefs shape Lucy's interactions with others, her view of herself, and her capacity to realize her potential. She feels trapped by self-imposed limitations.

• Isolation: Lucy feels disconnected from meaningful human connections. She perceives herself as an outsider, longing for connection but held back by the barriers of her beliefs.

By understanding the key components of our story, we gain insight into how our belief system—the narratives we tell ourselves about who we are, the world, and others—shapes the challenges we face. Unfolding these stories can help us access power, self-expression, happiness, freedom, and more.

In Lucy's story, her beliefs carry immense weight: shame, fear, anger, loneliness, anxiety, and possibly depression. These emotions affect her daily life, while beliefs like "I am tainted, unworthy, and unwanted" consume her thoughts, shaping her self-perception and internal struggles. Lucy's demeanor reflects her inner turmoil.

She walks with a hunched posture, avoids eye contact, hides behind her hair, and struggles to communicate. These beliefs limit every aspect of her life, from her interactions to her self-image and opportunities. Trapped by self- imposed limitations, Lucy feels profoundly isolated, like an outsider longing for connection but unable to bridge the gap.

Yet, by dismantling this narrative, Lucy opens the door to change. Understanding the origins of her beliefs gives her the power to challenge and rewrite them, replacing self-limiting thoughts with empowering ones. This transformation allows her to reshape her self-perception, unlock her potential, and create a life aligned with her goals.

BELIEFS:
THE LENS THAT WARPS OUR WORLD

Beliefs have the incredible power to shape our reality. They act as lenses through which we perceive the world, influencing how we interpret events, interactions, and even our own identity.

As we grow and encounter life's challenges, these lenses become more complex, layering over time as our experiences deepen and expand.

What makes beliefs particularly compelling is how they often operate beneath the surface of our conscious awareness. These deep-seated convictions may feel like intrinsic parts of our personality or identity, yet they function as the silent architects of our thoughts, actions, and decisions. It's this subconscious influence that makes beliefs so impactful—they subtly dictate how we respond to the world without us realizing it.

Our personal stories, built on the foundation of these beliefs, begin in childhood. These stories are shaped by how we interpret pivotal moments, such as rejection, failure, or unmet expectations. Each incident contributes to the narrative we create about ourselves, others, and life itself. By adulthood, these stories have grown into intricate frameworks, guiding our perceptions and behaviors.

Take a moment to consider the power of these beliefs. They dictate whether we feel capable or incapable, worthy or unworthy, and loved or unloved. They influence how we approach challenges, relationships, and opportunities. They form the roots of our inner dialogue—the voice that tells us what we can or cannot achieve. And like branches of a tree, they grow outward, affecting every facet of our lives.

Understanding this process of belief formation is crucial. When we become aware of how our beliefs are shaping our reality, we gain the ability to challenge and reframe them. This awareness is the first step toward reclaiming our agency—choosing to see the world not through the lens of limitation, but through one of possibility and growth.

In the next section, we'll explore how this awareness can lead to transformation. By examining the origins of our beliefs and their influence on our lives, we can begin to rewrite our stories and align our actions with our true potential.

PART 2

3

SHAPED BY BELIEFS

CHAPTER SIX:

THE JOHNNY STORY:
BOUND BY 'NEVER EVER'

Think back to Johnny's story—a five-year-old boy experiencing rejection for the first time. Eager to share his report card, he bursts into his dad's office, shouting, "Daddy, Daddy, look what I got!"

But his dad, absorbed in work, responds curtly, "Johnny, I am busy! Not now!" Johnny's excitement is replaced by confusion and heartbreak. The warmth and approval he had anticipated vanish in an instant, replaced by feelings of rejection. That painful moment shaped his beliefs, influencing how he saw himself and others.

In that instant, Johnny made a decision: "NEVER, EVER again..." Determined to avoid feeling small or unimportant, he shut himself off emotionally.

This belief, born from disappointment, would go on to shape his interactions and self-perception. Take a moment to reflect: Have you ever made a "NEVER, EVER" decision? These declarations often stem from moments of hurt or frustration, shaping our outlook and actions.

Here are some examples of restrictive "NEVER, EVER" statements:

- I will never ever trust.
- I will never ever love again.
- I will never ever ask for help.
- I will never ever forgive.
- I will never ever share my feelings.

While some "NEVER, EVER" statements hold us back, others empower us to move forward, such as:

- I will never ever quit.
- I will never ever lose hope.
- I will never ever stop striving for excellence.
- I will never ever let fear hold me back.

What are your "NEVER, EVER" statements? Recognizing these declarations helps us understand the stories we tell ourselves—and whether they limit us or motivate us.

When someone declares, "I will never, ever," it is often a way to shield themselves from future pain or disappointment. However, in doing so, they may unknowingly form beliefs that shape their perspective and limit their actions. Let's hear from Johnny about his own "never ever" decision.

Narrator: Johnny, what is it that you will never ever do?
Johnny: I have decided to never share my happiness or accomplishments with my family or friends.
Narrator: Why?
Johnny: Because when I tried to share my joy with my father, he showed no interest. It left me feeling unimportant, insignificant, and worthless. I started to believe that nobody cares and the world is harsh.
Narrator: So, what drives this decision?
Johnny: I believe that sharing leads to disappointment and rejection. To avoid feeling small and insignificant, I've chosen to never bother again.

Johnny's decision to stop sharing his happiness has far-reaching effects. He avoids pursuing accomplishments or embracing success, and his once bright and lively spirit is overshadowed by disappointment. The joyful boy who sought connection is now weighed down by his belief in his own insignificance.

AFTER THE
'NEVER EVER' COMES THE 'BECAUSE'

So Johnny has decided to never again (and what follows is the action of sharing or enjoyin his achievemnets or expecting attention). Then Comes the reason for "never again sharing or enjoying his achievements or expecting attention": the "becuse."

The reason Johnny gives after the "because" explains why he made the "never agin" declaration. This strong commitment to "never again" is not random; it has a justification. Including the word "because" helps clarity the motives gehind this decision.

Understanding this connectin is crucial, as it allows you to recognize whether there is a belief tied to that "because"--and, often, there is. So, how will Johnyy behave after adopting the belief that he doesn't matter? He will likely gegin to withdraw, distance himself from otheres, and may even become antisocial.

Just like Johnny, many of us have felt that emptiness, caused by various reasons. Often, we suppress these feelings and move on, but these emotions remain in our memorey, and if we don't confront them, they can resurface and create difficulties in our lives.

Take Johnny's mother, Sophia, for example. Raised in a foster home, she endured mistreatment that led her to believe, "I am unworthy and unclean." This belief haunted her throughout her life.

Similarly, Johnny's father, Joe, grew up with an abusive, alcoholic father. Joe's childhood promises to "never let my children go hungry" drove him to work tirelessly as a provider, but it left him emotionally unavailable to his son.

His "never ever" commitment to material support overshadowed his ability to provide emotional connection.Johnny eventually came to understand that his parents' actions were shaped by their own limiting beliefs and experiences. Just as he was confined by his belief system, so were they.

He could see that his parents' "never ever" rules—whether to avoid connection, vulnerability, or authenticity—were born from fear of pain and disappointment.

It's only by understanding these patterns that we can begin to dismantle the cycles of fear and create healthier relationships with ourselves and others.

BELIEFS & FEAR: THE CYCLE OF SELF PROTECTION

Life's experiences leave lasting marks, shaping how we view ourselves and the world. Often, fear arises as a response, rooted in beliefs we've formed.

For instance, a fear of speaking might stem from the belief, "People will find me ridiculous." This belief influences behavior, limiting self-expression.

Fear is a natural, protective instinct designed to keep us safe. However, when driven by beliefs, fear can become excessive, holding us back from taking action, expressing ourselves, or pursuing what matters.

For example, Johnny's belief that he doesn't matter made him afraid to share happiness with others or rely on those he saw as more important. These beliefs, tied to fear, shaped his behavior and limited his connections.

Unhealthy fears, fueled by limiting beliefs, restrict our potential. They hinder action, self- expression, and personal growth. Below are common fears and the beliefs that often underlie them:

1. Fear of Failure
Driven by the belief that failure defines worthlessness, leading to avoidance of risks and perfectionism.

2. Fear of Rejection
Rooted in the belief that rejection confirms personal inadequacy, causing low self-esteem.

3. Fear of Being Alone
Based on the belief that aloneness equates to loneliness or unhappiness, resulting in dependence on others.

4. Fear of Public Speaking
Tied to beliefs about judgment and performance anxiety, creating avoidance of opportunities.

5. Fear of Abandonment
Stemming from beliefs of being unlovable or flawed, leading to insecurity and clinginess.

6. Fear of Change
Fueled by beliefs that change brings loss or failure, causing resistance to new experiences.

7. Fear of the Unknown
Rooted in the belief that uncertainty is inherently risky, resulting in avoidance and anxiety.

8. Fear of Success
Influenced by feelings of unworthiness, leading to self-sabotage or fear of exposure.

9. Fear of Criticism
Driven by beliefs that criticism equals rejection or inadequacy, causing fear of feedback or vulnerability.

10. Fear of Taking Risks
Based on beliefs that risks are dangerous or threatening, leading to hesitation and missed opportunities.

11. Fear of Disappointment
Linked to beliefs that rejection or failure leads to emotional pain, fostering avoidance.

12. Fear of Mistakes
Stemmed from beliefs of inadequacy, driving perfectionism and fear of failure.

13. Fear of Being Judged
Rooted in the belief that worth depends on others' opinions, stifling authenticity.

14. Fear of Not Being Good Enough
Tied to self-doubt and unrealistic standards, leading to feelings of inadequacy.

15. Fear of Confrontation
Influenced by people-pleasing tendencies and fear of rejection, causing avoidance of conflict.

16. Fear of Vulnerability
Rooted in past emotional pain or fear of judgment, leading to self-protection and emotional withdrawal.

Understanding these fears and their underlying beliefs is the first step toward breaking free from self-imposed limitations.

Recognizing how beliefs shape fears allow us to challenge them and embrace opportunities for growth and self-expression.

PART 3

THE EMOTIONAL MENU

PART 3

CHAPTER SEVEN:

DISCOVERING
FEAR THROUGH "WHY"

Fear often stems from deeply held beliefs. Asking "why" can help uncover the root of these fears and bring clarity to what holds us back. Below are examples of how exploring "why" can reveal the beliefs driving common fears:

- Why am I afraid of speaking?
Because I believe people will find me ridiculous.

- Why am I afraid of laughing?
Because I think my teeth are unattractive and feel self-conscious.

- Why am I afraid of the dark?
Because I fear my abuser might reappear.

- Why am I afraid of being seen?
Because I believe I look funny or unusual.

- Why am I afraid of wearing makeup?
Because I think it's only for conventionally attractive women.

- Why am I afraid of answering the phone?
Because I worry, I won't understand what's being said.

- Why am I afraid of having children?
Because I believe the world is too unpleasant to bring them into.

- Why am I afraid to participate in class?
Because I think my answers aren't impressive enough.

- Why am I afraid to ask for what I want?
Because I feel unworthy or undeserving.

- Why do I always get last place?
Because I believe I'm not wanted or valued by others.

- Why am I afraid of failing? 57
Because I fear disappointing others.

- Why am I afraid to be out in public?
Because I think I'm not attractive enough.

Why is understanding the root causes of our fears important? Because it makes it easier to address and overcome them. By identifying these causes, you can approach them with clarity and tackle them effectively. When answering "why," it often begins with "I am afraid of," followed by "because." The statement after "because" reveals the underlying force driving your fear.

Use the following prompts to identify your fears:

- I am afraid of — because —
- I am afraid of — because —
- I am afraid of — because —

Thank you for participating in this exercise.

Next, let's explore how Johnny's accumulation of fears and beliefs shapes his journey into adulthood.

PART 3

Before Johnny's experience of disappointment, he was a diligent student with excellent grades. However, following his first major setback, his academic performance declined. His grades dropped, he became disengaged in class, and he isolated himself during playtime, preferring solitude.

One day, Johnny's father receives a call from his teacher requesting a meeting to discuss Johnny's behavior and performance. At the meeting, the teacher highlights the stark contrast between Johnny's previous success and his recent struggles. She expresses concern and asks if the parents are aware of any issues at home that could explain the change.

Johnny's mother reassures the teacher that everything is fine, while his father remains silent, lost in thought.

The parents pledge to observe Johnny more closely and work with the teacher to address his challenges.

However, when Johnny returns home, his father confronts him harshly, expressing disappointment and emphasizing the importance of education. Instead of a compassionate conversation, his father's words reinforce Johnny's belief that he is insignificant, labeling him as a potential "loser" or "failure."

Overwhelmed, Johnny retreats to his room, locking the door behind him. Alone, he internalizes his father's remarks, adding to his negative self-image: "I am a loser," "I don't matter," and "I am alone." These beliefs deepen his sense of isolation and his view of the world as harsh and unkind.

THE
DISSAPOINTMENT DEEPENS

Four years have passed, it is Saturday afternoon, and Johnny has a baseball game that he very excited about. His mom is taking him, but deep down, he longed for his father's presence.

Despite being aware of his father's busy schedule, Johnny mustered up the courage to ask him, "Dad, I know you're busy, but would you like to be at my game today?"

His father's deep affection for him shone through, as he lovingly promised to be there, making Johnny's heart soar with joy.

After Johnny and his mom arrived at the game, his mom made her way to the stands while Johnny headed to the locker room and then to the field to warm up.

As Johnny was going through his warm-up routine on the field, he periodically glances towards the benches, hoping to spot his dad.

However, he only sees his mom sitting there. Despite the absence of his father, Johnny reassured himself, thinking, "There's still time," and continued with his warm-up.

The game is about to begin, and his dad has still not arrived. Johnny's heart raced with a mix of excitement for the game and anxiety because his dad was nowhere to be seen on the benches.

Time passed, and as the game reached its halfway point, his dad still hadn't shown up. Eventually, the game ended, and much to Johnny's disappointment, his dad never appeared.

"This is truly disheartening," he thought to himself. Seeing his dad's absence at the game served as evidence, in his mind, that his dad didn't care about him.

In that moment, he found himself further reinforcing the belief

he already held about himself – that he was alone, on his own, and that he didn't matter or hold significance.

As life continues to unfold, much like in the case of Lucy and Johnny, our personal stories shaped by our beliefs expand progressively. We consistently integrate new beliefs into our belief system, and these beliefs subsequently influence the decisions we make, ultimately governing the course of our lives.

Our beliefs, whether starting with 'I am,' 'they are,' or 'the world is,' have the power to shape our perspectives on ourselves, others, and the world around us.

The 'I am' beliefs may take the form of 'I am not important,' 'I am not enough,' 'I am not lovable,' 'I am ugly,' 'I am fat,' 'I am poor,' 'I am unwanted,' 'I am unacceptable,' 'I am second choice,' 'I am dumb,' and the list goes on.

The 'they are' beliefs might include statements like 'they are cruel,' 'they are mean,' 'they are rude,' 'they don't care,' 'they are beasts,' and so forth.

These beliefs then extend to our perception of the world, with thoughts such as 'the world is harsh,' 'the world is not interested in kids,' 'the world is cruel,' 'the world is empty,' 'the world is full of mean people,' 'the world is tough,' 'the world is a dark place,' and more.

Take a moment to reflect and write down any of these beliefs that resonate with you, as you summarize your personal story:

Start with "I AM"
then "THEY ARE" and
Finally: "THE WORLD IS"

I AM:

_____

_____

_____

_____

THEY ARE

_____

_____

_____

_____

PART 3

THE WORLD IS

When someone makes statements like 'I am,' 'they are,' or 'the world is,' those statements become declarations, which have substantial power. Here are a few examples of declarations...

1. I am capable of achieving my goals.
2. They are supportive and loving.
3. The world is full of opportunities.
4. I am deserving of happiness and success.
5. They are kind-hearted and compassionate.
6. The world is abundant in resources.
7. I am confident in my abilities.
8. They are trustworthy and reliable.
9. The world is a place of growth and learning.
10. I am worthy of love and respect.
11. They are understanding and empathetic.
12. The world is filled with beauty and diversity.
13. I am resilient and can overcome challenges.
14. They are honest and genuine.
15. The world is a source of inspiration and creativity.

Declarations can have a powerful impact on our mindset and actions.

When Johnny said, 'I am,' 'they are,' and 'the world is,' it became a declaration for him in his mind; and as we will see these declarations, had significant power later in his life.

We are not fully conscious of the beliefs or statements we are forming within ourselves. This lack of awareness prevents us from understanding the impact these declarations will have on our life, how they will shift our thoughts, emotions, feelings and actions.

In essence, we are unaware of the power held by these internal statements in shaping our perception of ourselves, others, and the world. Johnny wasn't aware of the thoughts and beliefs he had in his mind.

He didn't realize how these thoughts and beliefs affected his life, changing the way he thought, felt, and acted.

Because of this, Johnny didn't understand how powerful his own thoughts were in shaping how he saw himself, others, and the world. He didn't realize that his thoughts had a big impact on his perception of everything around him.

Unaware of it, Johnny has unknowingly trapped himself by declaring, 'I am not important, I am insignificant, I am a loser, I am a failure,' and 'I don't matter.'

By using Johnny's sentence declarations as an example, you might be able to identify certain things you have told yourself, the sentences you have created about who you are.

Take a moment to reflect and write them down in the provided space. These sentences can be either positive or negative; the important thing is for you to distinguish them.

Take a moment to write them down.

_____

_____

_____

_____

The following is a list of limiting beliefs that often take the form of a declaration.

1. I'm not good enough, they are scary, life is too hard, they don't like me.

2. I am too tall, I am too short, I am not pretty, I am not able, it is too hard.

3. I am not deserving, the world is harsh, I will fail, I am not intelligent enough.

4. I am not lovable, I am unwanted, I am no fun, I am I don't deserve success.

5. They make fun of me, I'll never be successful, I will always lack.

6. I will never finish this task, it is too hard, I am overweight.

7. Overweight is ugly, I am not pretty enough to be a model.

8. They look better than me, I am not smart/talented/creative enough.

These are just a few declarations, but there are too many to count. Everyone is unique, and each person has their own declarations that shape their perspective.

Johnny also expressed judgments about his parents when he believed they didn't care and were emotionally unavailable.

Have you also formed similar judgments about your own parents or caregivers?

Take a moment to write them down.

_____
_____
_____
_____

You may have observed that Johnny also expressed judgment about the world by saying, 'the world is harsh.' If you have made any declarations or judgments about the world or life, please write them down below.

_____
_____
_____
_____

After making a declaration, we unconsciously align ourselves with it, leading to our demeanor, behavior, and actions reflecting those self-imposed declarations.

This alignment with self-imposed declarations can indeed influence our state of mind. These sentences that we declare stay in our subconscious and may resurface later in life without any clear explanation.

They keep recurring and causing discomfort, persisting over time when awakened by something in the environment. We will use the terms "alarms" or "triggers" to refer to that which awakens the sentences, as they are alarming in nature and prompt us to enter into survival mode.

TRIGGERS AND
SURVIVAL MECHANISMS

Triggers are situations, words, or any stimulus that elicits an intense emotional or psychological reaction within us, usually negative, associated with past experiences.

These triggers can make us feel threatened or vulnerable and, as a result, lead us to automatic responses, such as avoiding the situation, feeling anxiety, anger, or resorting to defense mechanisms.

When these triggers appear, they evoke a survival response within us, which in turn moves us into action. We promptly begin seeking refuge or finding comfort.

When Johnny is triggered, he is simply being reminded of his deeply held beliefs. In response, he resorts to his survival mechanism, which involves seeking comfort through food and isolation.

He may start binge-eating and retreat to a secluded place with a bucket of ice cream or other binge-worthy foods.

Many of us turn to comfort zones or coping mechanisms without fully understanding why. Here's a list of common comfort zones or survival mechanisms that people often resort to when triggered:

1. Emotional eating or overeating.

2. Social withdrawal or isolation.

3. Excessive use of technology or screens.

4. Substance abuse or addiction.

5. Engaging in obsessive or compulsive behaviors.

6. Avoidance or procrastination.

7. Seeking constant validation or approval from others.

8. Busy-ness or overworking.

9. Escaping through entertainment or distractions.

10. Self-sabotage or self-destructive behaviors.

When Johnny resorted to eating and binging as a response to his triggers, he initially felt good and comfortable. However, afterwards he didn't feel as good. This is because seeking temporary comfort through actions that are not aligned with your true self is merely a survival mechanism.

Remember, these patterns of comfort-seeking can look different for everyone, and this list is just a starting point. We'll refer to this list as the 'pattern'—a set of behaviors you turn to whenever you're triggered, seeking comfort.

As we move forward, we'll explore how these patterns evolve into habits. Though they may provide temporary safety or comfort, they don't reflect who you truly are.

Why is this significant?

Because it leads us to our next topic: HABITS.

PART 3

How are habits formed? Do they also stem from underlying beliefs? In the upcoming chapter, we will delve into the nature of habits and explore these questions.

CHAPTER EIGHT:

HABITS & LIMITING BELIEFS:
A VICIOUS CYCLE

Have you ever heard the expression 'you are a creature of habit'? What exactly do people mean when they say that? This statement suggests that individuals tend to develop consistent patterns of behavior or routines in their daily lives.

It implies that habits play a significant role in shaping our actions, decisions, and overall lifestyle. In other words, it highlights the notion that humans have a natural tendency to fall into repetitive behaviors or routines that become ingrained and familiar over time.

These habits can influence various aspects of our lives, including how we think, act, and interact with others. Exploring the concept of being a 'creature of habit' can provide insights into the power of habits and their impact on our daily lives.

It is a common understanding among psychologists, behaviorists, and experts in habit formation that habits can vary in terms of their impact on our well-being.

Some habits, such as exercising regularly or practicing mindfulness, are considered healthy or beneficial. Unhealthy habits, on the other hand, could include smoking, excessive consumption of junk food, or procrastination. Neutral habits may refer to routines or behaviors that have minimal positive or negative impact on our lives, such as brushing our teeth or tying shoelaces in a particular way.

Here are some examples of neutral habits:

1. Brushing your teeth twice a day.

2. Making your bed in the morning.

3. Folding your clothes a certain way.

4. Checking your email or social media at a specific time.

5. Organizing your workspace before starting work.

6. Taking the same route to work or school.

7. Having a particular morning or bedtime routine.

8. Using specific gestures or phrases while communicating.

9. Tapping your foot or drumming your fingers when idle.

10. Keeping items in a specific order or arrangement.

Neutral habits are often routines or behaviors that we perform without much conscious thought or intention, and they don't necessarily have a significant positive or negative impact on our lives. A good habit is a behavior or routine that contributes positively to your well-being, productivity, and overall quality of life.

Good habits are typically intentional, beneficial, and aligned with your goals and values. They promote personal growth, physical health, mental well- being, and success in various areas of life.

EXAMPLES
OF GOOD HABITS

Examples of good habits include regular exercise, healthy eating, practicing gratitude, and effective time management.

The following are some additional examples of good habits:

1. Regular exercise or physical activity.

2. Practicing mindfulness or meditation.

3. Eating a balanced and nutritious diet.

4. Getting enough sleep and maintaining a consistent sleep schedule.

5. Reading books or learning new things regularly.

6. Setting and working towards achievable goals.

7. Prioritizing and managing time effectively.

8. Practicing gratitude and expressing appreciation.

9. Keeping a journal or practicing self-reflection.

10. Maintaining a clean and organized living space.

These are just a few examples, and good habits can vary depending on individual preferences and goals. The key is to cultivate habits that support your well-being, personal growth, and desired outcomes in different aspects of your life.

On the other hand, bad habits are those that have negative consequences or hinder our progress. These habits can be harmful to our health, productivity, relationships, or personal development.

EXAMPLES
OF BAD HABITS

Examples of bad habits include procrastination, excessive screen time, smoking, unhealthy eating, or negative self-talk.

The following are some additional examples of bad habits:

1. Procrastination: Delaying or postponing tasks until the last minute, leading to stress and poor time management.

2. Excessive screen time: Spending excessive amounts of time on electronic devices, such as smartphones, tablets, or computers, which can negatively impact productivity, sleep, and social interactions.

3. Unhealthy eating habits: Consuming excessive junk food, sugary drinks, or processed foods, which can lead to weight gain, poor nutrition, and various health issues.

4. Nail biting: Habitually biting or chewing nails, which can lead to damage to the nails and surrounding skin, and may indicate underlying anxiety or stress.

5. Smoking: Regularly smoking tobacco products, which can have detrimental effects on health and increase the risk of various diseases.

6. Excessive alcohol consumption: Consuming alcohol in excessive amounts or on a regular basis, which can have negative effects on physical and mental health, relationships, and overall well-being.

7. Negative self-talk: Engaging in constant self-criticism, negative thoughts, and self-doubt, which can erode self-esteem and hinder personal growth.

8. Excessive spending: Engaging in impulsive or unnecessary shopping, leading to financial strain and potential debt.

9. Lack of exercise: Failing to engage in regular physical activity or leading a sedentary lifestyle, which can contribute to various health issues and decreased energy levels.

WHY ARE
HABITS HARD TO BREAK?

Let's explore the reasons why breaking habits can be challenging. What defines a habit, and what factors contribute to their resistance to change or breaking?

A habit, as defined by The Britannica dictionary, is a recurring pattern of behavior or way of being that becomes customary or automatic. It involves engaging in an activity regularly, often without conscious awareness.

In essence, a habit is a repeated action, a pattern that emerges from performing something multiple times. Once an action is done repeatedly, it becomes a recognizable pattern or habit. A habit can be challenging to break due to several reasons.

First, habits are often deeply ingrained in our subconscious mind through repetition, making them automatic and effortless. They become deeply wired neural pathways in the brain, making it the default response in certain situations.

When we reflect on Johnny and Lucy's stories, it's clear that they didn't simply decide once that they were defective due to the beliefs and decisions formed after the incidents.

They kept thinking about it repeatedly, which made those decisions even stronger and more powerful over time. Not only that, but as they experienced more incidents, their viewpoints, perceptions, and beliefs expanded, incorporating new perspectives into how they saw themselves, the world, and others.

This addition of new perspectives added more sentences to their belief system, making the moments of discomfort stronger and more intense.

Even though the incidents themselves were long gone and in the past, the memories associated with them remained vivid and alive.

They lingered within their minds, playing out like reruns of a movie.

Whenever something triggered their memory of those incidents, their perception of the events felt as real and alive as ever, further reinforcing their beliefs. These recurring memories continued to strengthen and intensify those beliefs over time.

And even though there may be times when we are not even aware of the specific beliefs triggering these uncomfortable feelings, as these recurring beliefs resurface over time, they serve as reminders of the discomfort we originally experienced.

This lack of awareness leaves us uncertain about the origin of these feelings and why they persist. As these beliefs persist, we are compelled to do everything in our power to avoid the discomfort. We seek refuge and comfort, instinctively gravitating towards what feels safer and more comforting. And the place we turn to for safety and comfort is often a familiar one, as we have sought solace there before.

And this repetitive behavior is what we refer to as a pattern, which ultimately becomes a habit. Therefore, at the core of a habit lies a belief. Now that we have established this, let's explore the recurring behaviors that Johnny exhibited when triggered and experiencing discomfort.

DISTRESSING MOMENTS:
Feeling anxious, overwhelmed and out of place.

POSSIBLE TRIGGERS:
Feeling unimportant, like he doesn't matter, a loser/failure.

COMFORTING MECHANISMS:
Eating, binging, isolating, going to an alone place.

REPETITIVE BEHAVIOR:
Eating, binging, isolating, going to an alone place.

Similar to Johnny, share your personal experiences of discomfort, triggers, and comforting mechanisms.

PART 3

DISTRESSING MOMENTS:

_____
_____
_____
_____

POSSIBLE TRIGGERS:

_____
_____
_____
_____

COMFORTING MECHANISMS:

_____
_____
_____
_____

REPETITIVE BEHAVIOR:

_____
_____
_____
_____

As we declare our beliefs or sentences, they prompt us to seek comfort, which in turn becomes a habit. Habits, in turn, yield results.

The type of habit determines the kind of results we obtain. Good habits lead to desired outcomes, while bad habits lead to unwanted outcomes.

Take a moment to reflect on the results you are experiencing. Are they desired or undesired results?

Identify the habit that is generating the undesirable results.

_____
_____
_____
_____

Keep in mind that all of this takes place internally and has the power to shape our perspectives, emotions, and behaviors.

Different individuals have their own ways of manifesting their survival mechanisms. Some may find distraction through watching TV, rely on smoking, turn to excessive eating or drinking, engage in running or sports, seek escape through sleeping, or even resort to drugs, some of which can have detrimental consequences.

In Johnny's case, his repetitive behavior of eating and binge-ing resulted in weight gain, reaching a staggering 300 pounds. This weight gain brought about feelings of fatigue, sickness, overwhelm, and discomfort in his own body. Clearly, these were not desirable results.

SUMMARY:

In summary, habits stem from underlying beliefs. Therefore, we can conclude that, for the most part, the belief is already, and the habit follows. We tend to seek our comfort zone whenever we feel unsafe, insecure, or vulnerable, often without realizing it.

This repeated action forms a pattern, which eventually be-comes a habit. Imagine experiencing a moment that prompts us to seek refuge and comfort, as it triggers a memory from the past.

This memory, stored in our minds, resurfaces when something triggers it, leading us to instinctively seek comfort and safety.

As this memory continues to be triggered and resurfaces re-peatedly, the comfort-seeking behavior transforms into a habit through repetition.

Once formed it will possibly be hard to break. Breaking a habit means disrupting the comfort and facing uncertainty, which can be uncomfortable and even anxiety-inducing, despite habits often serving a purpose or fulfilling a need by providing comfort, satisfaction, or a sense of familiarity. However, in most cases, they lead to undesired results.

As you can see, habits are often associated with cues or triggers in our environment, which can reignite the urge to engage in the habit. Breaking a habit requires identifying and addressing these triggers, which demands self-awareness, effort, and conscious decision-making.

Additionally, habits can become deeply intertwined with our identity and self-perception. Letting go of a habit may challenge our sense of who we are, resulting in resistance or fear of change. Therefore, breaking a habit requires not only addressing the external triggers but also confronting the internal factors that influence our behaviors and self-image.

Overall, breaking a habit requires awareness, commitment, and a willingness to face discomfort and make conscious choices to develop new patterns of behavior.

With this in mind we can dive into our next part where we will discuss how Jimmy was able to break some of his strongest habits. Let's dive in.

4

BECOMING GREATER THAN YOUR ENVIRONMENT

CHAPTER NINE: THE JIMMY STORY

Previously we learned that certain fears based on beliefs when triggered cause us discomfort, which in turn lead us to instinctively seek comfort. In time we develop our own comfort zones or survival mechanisms that later turn into habits.

These patterns unconsciously influence our behavior. To uncover the roots of these discomforting moments, we must embrace discomfort and observe the thoughts that arise. Through self-reflection, we gain insight into the underlying factors contributing to our discomfort.

Jimmy was a bright and intelligent young boy. However, his early years were marked by unfortunate events. After his father left, Jimmy's mother remarried without realizing that her new husband had a tendency to bully others. Tragically, Jimmy became a victim of his stepfather's abusive behavior, both physically and verbally, on a regular basis.

One particular incident stands out: his stepfather forced him to unclog a toilet using his bare hands.

Imagine this young boy, plunging his hands into the filth, removing everything that had accumulated there. It's hard to comprehend the emotions he must have felt in that moment. Not only was he subjected to verbal abuse, ridicule, and scorn, but he was also forced to carry out physically degrading tasks.

The continuous mistreatment instilled a sense of hopelessness and powerlessness in him, as he internalized the bully's derogatory remarks and abusive behavior.

That environment, characterized by the presence of the bully, plays a significant role in shaping Jimmy's perception and interpretation of the world around him.

As he absorbs the sights and sounds of his surroundings, he forms interpretations based on his own perspective, which in turn influences his actions and emotions.

In a way, he is being conditioned and influenced by his environment.

When Jimmy enters his teenage years, he finds himself grappling with anxiety attacks that occur in various settings, such as school, field games, and even at home while watching TV.

Despite having received treatment for his trauma in the past, Jimmy remains dissatisfied with the explanations he has been given for these anxious episodes.

Determined to find answers and regain control over his life, Jimmy takes on the role of a self-appointed detective.

To embark on his personal investigation, Jimmy starts documenting every move and action he takes, with particular attention to the events or surroundings that trigger his anxiety. This meticulous record-keeping allows him to identify patterns and potential triggers that he may have overlooked before.

Through this process, he hopes to gain a deeper understanding of his anxiety and uncover the underlying reasons behind it. With a detective-like mindset, Jimmy becomes attuned to the subtleties of his daily life. He pays close attention to his thoughts, emotions, and physical sensations, noting how they relate to specific situations or experiences.

By connecting the dots between his documented observations and his anxiety attacks, Jimmy gradually pieces together a clearer picture of the factors contributing to his distress.

In addition to his personal documentation, Jimmy also explores external resources. He delves into books, articles, and online forums, searching for information and insights that resonate with his experiences. He discovers coping strategies, relaxation techniques, and self- care practices that may help manage anxiety.

Engaging with others who have faced similar challenges, Jimmy finds a sense of community and support, realizing he is not alone in his struggle.

Jimmy's determination to play detective in his own life allows him to gain a deeper understanding of himself and his anxiety. As he unravels the intricate web of triggers and responses, he gradually develops a personalized toolkit of coping mechanisms to mitigate his anxious episodes.

With his newfound self-awareness, Jimmy discovers that certain events or situations trigger intense memories from his past, causing him ot relive emotions and sensations that connect his present to those experiences.

Let's take a look—it is 1998, June, Saturday afternoon.

WHEN TRIGGERS
AWAKEN MEMORIES

As Jimmy enters the soccer field on a Saturday afternoon, the atmosphere is filled with excitement and anticipation. The crowd gathers, eagerly awaiting the start of the game.

However, something unexpected happens to Jimmy. Out of the blue, he experiences a sudden rush of anxiety, his heart races, his muscles tense up and his palms become sweaty as if his body is responding to an imminent danger that only he perceives.

Amidst the crowd's excitement, Jimmy's inner turmoil intensifies. All he wants is to escape, to flee from the soccer field and find solace in solitude. The urge to run away and hide grows stronger within him, as if seeking refuge from the overwhelming pressure and scrutiny that he perceives around him. Has that ever happened to you?

It doesn't have to be as drastic as Jimmy's dramatic scene, but have you ever had a moment of uncertainty that impacted your ability to fully express or feel free to be yourself.

A moment of shyness that made you feel self-conscious and hinder the ability to speak up or engage with others. Or a temporary loss of confidence that limited you from speaking in your own natural way.

It's important to remember that everyone goes through these moments to some degree. While these experiences might not be as drastic as the dramatic scene Jimmy experienced, they can still have an impact on a person's inner strength and self-expression. Overcoming such moments often involves building confidence, and self-awareness.

Easier said than done, but by recognizing and understanding these moments, we can work towards regaining our inner strength and expressing ourselves more fully in the future. How do we do that?

By identifying what the triggers are—we must first identify what trigger the body sensations, what triggered the sweating in the

case of Jimmy, what lead to this uninvited moment. Once we learn to identify we can start building inner strength. If you've ever found yourself in a disagreeable space where you wanted to run and hide, becoming aware of the moment can be a helpful first step.

PART 4

Take a moment to reflect on your own experiences and choose one incident in which you were in a disagreeable state. Record your thoughts on paper.

Here's an illustration of how you could approach it:

Body sensations: My heart starts pounding rapidly, and I feel a tightness in my chest. My palms become sweaty, and I can feel a knot forming in my stomach.

Thoughts: Thoughts of self-doubt and worry flood my mind. I start questioning my abilities and fearing judgment from others. Negative thoughts like "I can't handle this" or "I'm going to embarrass myself" consume my thinking.

Feelings: Overwhelm washes over me, and I begin to feel anxious and vulnerable. There's a strong urge to escape the situation, seeking safety and comfort elsewhere. I might feel a sense of helplessness or a desire to withdraw from social interaction.

Remember, these experiences can vary from person to person. It's important to acknowledge and validate your own unique feelings and reactions.

- Body Sensations: —————————
- Thoughts: ————————
- Feelings: ————————
- Details of the Moment: ————————
- Where are you? ————————
- Who is there? —————————
- What time is it? (Day, evening, afternoon, or morning?) —
- What are you doing? —————
- When did it happen? ———————————————-

Jimmy has experienced this situation multiple times before; it is not the first occurrence. However, the source of this anxiety remains unknown, leaving Jimmy perplexed and caught off guard. In this moment of distress, Jimmy longs for a sense of safety and relief.

PART 4

He yearns to find a space where he can gather his thoughts, regain composure, and confront the anxiety that has unexpectedly gripped him. It's a struggle between the desire to participate in the game and the overwhelming urge to retreat and seek shelter.

When Jimmy grapples with his inner turmoil, it becomes important for him to find ways to manage his anxiety. As he gains control of the situation, he runs to the place where he knows he can regroup and gather his thoughts, the bathroom.

Inside the bathroom, Jimmy's panic symptoms likely intensified, leading to freezing behavior, characterized by feeling immobilized or unable to take action.

Freezing is a common response during moments of extreme anxiety or fear. Panicking and freezing alternated as he grappled with the overwhelming emotions and physical sensations associated with the panic attack. After practicing a set of breathing techniques, Jimmy employs them to regain control.

Once he attains a state of calmness, he directs his focus towards seeking answers. Jimmy will start to pay attention to his internal thoughts, dialogues and emotions at the time of the incident. "Am I experiencing any negative self-talk or self-doubt? Is there an underlying fear or worry that's contributing to this tension?" By examining his internal state, Jimmy can uncover any emotional triggers that might be playing a role in his current feelings.

This triggers at times can be so subtle, that even a seemingly insignificant stimuli can have a profound impact on an individual's emotional well-being and trigger unexpected reactions. That is not too easy to identify.

So, what specific event or circumstance caused Jimmy's panic attack to occur? Jimmy's world was peaceful until something so subtle that no one would ever suspect threw him into distress and confusion. What was it?

It was an eerily familiar voice, mirroring that of his stepfather, when the voice reached his ears. In that very moment, his emotional strength began to crumble. It was a voice that held a particular tone, one that instantly transported him back in time, as if a time machine had awakened his dormant memories.

It seemed to be coming from behind him. And it was so that caught him by surprise. It was as if that man was right behind him following him the profound effect on Jimmy's emotions was undeniable, evoking an overwhelming surge of fear and anxiety. It triggered an instinctual fight-or-flight response, overpowering his senses and ultimately leading to a panic attack.

After Jimmy discovers what triggered his anxiety, he experiences a sense of relief and understanding. However, he realizes that merely identifying the trigger is not enough for him to overcome his fear and find true satisfaction. He yearns to delve deeper into his past and uncover the precise moment when the fear of that haunting voice first took hold of him.

Driven by his curiosity and the desire to confront his fears head-on, Jimmy embarks on a journey of self-discovery.

REWIND TO
JIMMY'S YOUNGER YEARS

Jimmy reflects on a memory from his younger years when life seemed simpler—just him and his mother. At age seven, his mother remarried, and soon after, Jimmy faced verbal and physical abuse from his stepfather. One particular morning stands out in his mind. Jimmy was seated at the kitchen table, enjoying his favorite cereal, as sunlight streamed through the curtains, creating a serene atmosphere.

That peace was abruptly disrupted when his stepfather entered the room, commanding Jimmy to abandon his breakfast and clean the kitchen floor. The sharp tone of his stepfather's voice filled Jimmy with tension and dread, replacing the warmth of the morning with an overwhelming sense of obligation and fear. Eager to comply but struggling under the weight of impossible expectations, Jimmy reluctantly rose to complete the task.

Kneeling with a bucket of soap and water, Jimmy spent over an hour scrubbing the floor, only to have his efforts dismissed with criticism for a missed spot. His anticipation of praise turned to disappointment, reinforcing feelings of inadequacy and powerlessness.

This moment, etched deeply into his memory, became associated with his stepfather's harsh voice—a sound that made Jimmy tremble and freeze.

As Jimmy revisits this memory, he begins to notice patterns and recurring images that offer valuable clues about his anxiety. While identifying the trigger provides some relief, he realizes it is not enough to overcome his fear.

Determined to dig deeper, Jimmy embarks on a journey of self-discovery, tracing his fear back to its origins. He starts recognizing how moments of vulnerability and trauma shaped his responses, offering him a clearer understanding of himself and the roots of his unease.

In that moment, Jimmy realizes, "This is it! This is the moment I understand the bully doesn't care about the cleanliness of the floor. "He just wants to make me miserable because I am my mother's son."

This awareness becomes a crucial step in dismantling the grip that fear, and anxiety have held on to his life.

Jimmy reflects further: "Every time after that, when I heard his voice, I would run and hide, though he always found me. That voice became deeply ingrained in me, triggering my anxiety because I lived in constant fear of what he might do or demand next. It was the start of a miserable existence."

With the trigger clearly identified, Jimmy embarks on a journey to confront and reduce its influence. Through exploration and self-awareness, he uncovers strategies tailored to his needs, enabling him to reclaim control over his thoughts and emotions.

PART 4

Now, let's delve into the next chapter to explore these strategies in greater detail and understand how to effectively address and overcome anxiety triggers.

CHAPTER TEN:

TAKING A CLOSER LOOK
AT ANXIETY TRIGGERS

Understanding the root causes of anxiety or the factors that shaped who we are today requires a deep dive into our thoughts, feelings, and past experiences through introspection and self-reflection.

By carefully examining these aspects, we can uncover specific triggers and beliefs that influenced our self-perception and contributed to anxiety. This process provides valuable insights into the origins of our struggles and fosters personal growth.

Introspection and self-reflection are essential tools for identifying the exact triggers or beliefs behind anxiety and shaping our current selves.

The following are some suggestions to guide this process:

1. Reflect on triggering events:

Look back at moments that caused anxiety or shaped you. Recall times when you felt overwhelmed, stuck, or influenced in significant ways .

Take a moment to write them down.

_____

_____

_____

_____

2. Examine your reactions and emotions: Focus on how you felt during those moments. Did fear, shame, or self-doubt arise? Identifying emotions offers clues about beliefs you
hold about yourself.

_____

_____

_____

_____

3. Identify recurring patterns: Look for themes in triggering events. Are there situations that consistently cause anxiety? These patterns can reveal core beliefs shaping your self- perception.

_____

_____

_____

_____

4. Question your beliefs: Analyze the beliefs tied to your triggers. Why do you hold them? Are they based on facts or shaped by past distortions? Challenge and reframe them as needed.

_____

_____

_____

_____

Exploring deep-rooted beliefs can be challenging. If navigating this process feels overwhelming, seek guidance from trusted experts who can provide support and a safe space for exploration.

Remember, self-discovery and growth are ongoing. Be patient and compassionate as you reflect and embrace the chance to redefine yourself in alignment with your values and aspirations.

FAST-FORWARD TO JIMMY'S
PRESENT TIME AT THE GAME

Unraveling the precise moment in which Jimmy is wired to believe that he is hopeless and there nothing he can do, holds the key to unlocking profound insights that propels him forward on a path of growth.

By delving into the depths of this triggering FACTOR, Jimmy gains the ability to confront his anxiety head-on, armed with a fresh perspective.

You see, this is who Jimmy has become—a timid individual with a hint of rebelliousness. He cautiously takes one step forward, but often finds himself taking two steps back when he tries to pursue what he truly loves. In his pursuit, he has learned not to divulge too much about himself and to be wary of placing trust in others.

However, deep within him, there is a burning desire to achieve victory, to succeed in something meaningful. Despite his self-perceived insignificance, Jimmy holds onto an inner belief that he is somebody, not the nobody he often perceives himself to be.

Driven by this realization, Jimmy embarks on a transformative journey of self-discovery. He becomes increasingly aware that the environment he grew up in has played a significant role in shaping him—both his fears and aspirations.

With a burning curiosity, he seeks to understand the intricacies of how his surroundings have molded him into the person he is today.

By delving into this quest for self-awareness, Jimmy hopes to uncover the hidden facets of his identity, unearthing the untapped potential within him.

Through this journey, Jimmy confronts his fears, challenges his limitations, and embraces the unknown. He learns to question the beliefs and narratives that have shaped his perception of himself.

With each step he takes, Jimmy discovers new dimensions of his character, unravels his passions, and awakens the courage to pursue his dreams wholeheartedly.

This voyage of self-discovery is not without its obstacles, as Jimmy encounters setbacks, doubts, and moments of vulnerability. Yet, he perseveres, fueled by the profound realization that unlocking his true self will lead to a life of fulfillment and purpose.

Along the way, he seeks guidance from mentors, immerses himself in diverse experiences, and immerses himself in self- examination to gain a deeper understanding of who he truly is.

As Jimmy continues his journey, he gradually sheds the timidity that once held him back. He becomes bolder, more resilient, and unafraid to embrace his authentic self. The transformation he undergoes is not merely external, but a profound internal shift that redefines his outlook on life.

Ultimately, Jimmy's journey of self-discovery is a testament to the power of self-observation, growth, and the pursuit of one's true passions.

Through self-reflection and a willingness to challenge his own limitations, he emerges as a more confident, self-assured individual.

Armed with newfound self-belief and a clear sense of purpose, Jimmy sets out to conquer the world, knowing that he is capable of achieving greatness and leaving an indelible mark on the tapestry of his own life.

SHAPED BY THE ENVIRONMNET— BUT NOT DEFINED BY IT

Jimmy realizes that while his environment significantly shaped him, it does not define him. He reflects on how it influenced his character and begins to identify the key turning points.

PART 4

Before he started believing he was "hopeless and weak," Jimmy's life was full of happiness, dreams, and a playful spirit. He approached challenges with bravery, intelligence, and determination. His kind manners reflected his thoughtfulness, and his outgoing nature fostered strong relationships.

Jimmy's gratitude and appreciation for life's small moments defined him. This was who Jimmy was before self-doubt crept in—a vibrant and positive individual.

The Law of Attraction suggests that our predominant thoughts and beliefs shape the experiences we attract. Jimmy's initial negative beliefs, such as "I am hopeless and weak" and "There is nothing I can do," aligned with this principle, creating a cycle that reinforced these beliefs. These thoughts led to repeated situations where Jimmy felt powerless, solidifying his self-doubt and hindering his progress.

For instance, in pursuing his goal to become a successful player, his belief in being "helpless and powerless" prevented him from taking steps to improve, seek opportunities, or overcome obstacles. This belief system became a self-fulfilling prophecy, leaving him stuck and unmotivated.

Now, Jimmy is actively working to confront and overcome his anxiety. By identifying his triggers, he recreates situations that provoke anxiety to face them head-on. Instead of avoiding or suppressing these thoughts, he acknowledges them, allowing himself to process and understand their origins.

Through consistent practice, Jimmy diminishes the intensity of his triggers, regaining control over his emotions and breaking the cycle of anxiety.

Jimmy recognizes that unless he reshapes his recurring thought patterns, his environment will continue to influence him. He begins a transformative journey to actively reshape his thoughts and shift his environment.

First:

Jimmy pays close attention to the voice that says he is "hopeless and weak." The next time it appears, he allows it to be without fighting it. As he acknowledges its presence, he continues this practice until the fear and its influence diminish.

Second:

After acknowledging the voice, Jimmy responds: "Yes, I understand that you perceive me as weak and hopeless. Thank you for sharing. I acknowledge your statements." He repeats this response every time the voice arises until he conquers it entirely.

Through this process, Jimmy takes an empowered step toward re-shaping his reality and freeing himself from the constraints of his past beliefs.

WHAT
YOU RESIST PERSISTS

The phrase "what you resist persists" highlights an important principle in personal growth: when we fight against or try to suppress a situation, emotion, or problem, we often give it more power.

The energy we invest in resisting can unintentionally reinforce the very thing we wish to avoid.

Alternatively, acknowledging, accepting, and addressing the issue directly can often lead to resolution or transformation.

Examples of Resistance and Its Persistence:

1. Relationship Conflicts:

Imagine two people in conflict. If one partner resists discussing the issues by avoiding conversations or dismissing concerns, the tension builds, making resolution more difficult.

However, when they approach the conflict with open communication and a willingness to listen, the resistance lessens, and progress becomes possible.

2. Unwanted Emotions:

Suppose someone feels anxious about public speaking. If they try to suppress the anxiety by avoiding opportunities to speak, the fear only grows stronger. By gradually exposing themselves to public speaking and acknowledging their anxiety, they can begin to reduce its intensity and build confidence.

3. Health and Habits:

Consider someone trying to overcome procrastination. Resisting the task at hand by constantly avoiding or distracting themselves often increases stress and makes the task feel even more overwhelming. However, breaking the task into smaller steps and facing it head-on can ease the resistance and make progress manageable.

4. Childhood Beliefs:

A child told they're "not good enough" might resist this belief by striving for perfection. The more they fight the feeling of inadequacy, the more they reinforce its grip. Over time, this resistance becomes a cycle of self-doubt. However, by examining the root of this belief and challenging its validity, they can start to rewrite their narrative.

When Jimmy first encountered the voice in his head, it filled him with anxiety. His immediate reaction was to run and hide, hoping the voice would disappear. Each time the voice returned, Jimmy fought harder to resist it, repeating the same cycle.

Paradoxically, his resistance didn't silence the voice—it made it stronger. The more he tried to suppress or escape it, the more it persisted, becoming a habitual source of stress.

This is the essence of resistance: instead of resolving the issue, it can solidify its presence. In Jimmy's case, avoiding the voice gave it more power, feeding his fears and reinforcing his belief that he was helpless and weak. He realized that running from the voice wasn't solving anything.

Jimmy's breakthrough came when he decided to stop resisting. Instead of fighting the voice, he paused, acknowledged it, and faced it with curiosity. He thought, "What if I let this voice exist instead of trying to silence it?" By doing so, he began to see the voice for what it was: a reflection of past fears, not a truth about his present or future.

For example:

• When the voice said, "You're weak and hopeless," Jimmy responded calmly, "Thank you for your opinion, but I choose not to believe that anymore."

• When anxiety crept in, he would sit with it and say, "I hear you, but you don't define me."

Each time he acknowledged the voice without resisting it, its power diminished. This practice, while challenging, helped Jimmy reframe his beliefs and take control of his emotions.

This principle isn't just about Jimmy—it's something we all can apply. Whether it's fears, unwanted emotions, or persistent problems, resisting often makes things worse.

Here's a simple practice:

1. Pause and Acknowledge: Instead of fighting, take a moment to recognize the emotion, thought, or challenge you're facing.

2. Label It: Give it a name: "This is anxiety," "This is doubt," or "This is fear."

3. Sit With It: Allow it to exist without judgment. Breathe deeply and remind yourself, "This will pass."

4. Reframe It: Challenge the belief behind the resistance. Replace it with a constructive or empowering thought.

PART 4

For example:

- Fear of failure? Replace it with: "Failure is just a step toward growth."

- Fear of rejection? Remind yourself: "Rejection doesn't define my worth."

By shifting from resistance to acceptance, you can break free from the patterns that hold you back. Jimmy's journey shows that transformation begins when you stop fighting and start understanding.

ALLOWING IT TO BE, WITHOUT RESISTANCE

Jimmy will pay close attention to the voice when it appears, noting its statements ("You are dumb, you are worthless, you cannot do anything right") and becoming aware of how it affects him, including its impact on his body sensations.

Jimmy consciously avoids putting up resistance to the voice. Instead, he allows it to be. Allowing something to be means permitting a situation or thought to exist without interference or resistance. It involves adopting a mindset of non-resistance, letting things unfold naturally without trying to control or change them.

This approach means acknowledging the voice without judgment or suppression, embracing its presence while staying present in the moment.

By allowing the voice to exist, Jimmy practices full awareness, listening to his body and mind without engaging in a struggle. He neither agrees nor disagrees with the voice's statements but instead acknowledges its presence with acceptance.

Once Jimmy starts feeling at ease and the voice becomes less disturbing, he begins to rewire his brain by affirming:

"Jimmy, you are powerful. You hold the power to shape your inner being. Though you were influenced by your environment, it is now time for you to have some influence on what surrounds you."

If Jimmy can do this, then we are also capable of working through our own challenges. Let's pause for a moment and perform the exercise as Jimmy does:

1. Pay close attention to the thoughts related to the inner voice causing anxiety or limitations. What is it saying?

_____
_____
_____
_____

2. Once you're clear on what the voice is communicating, don't fight it. Allow it to be, acknowledging its presence without resistance. Continue until you feel at ease and free, or until the fear or disturbance lessens.

_____
_____
_____
_____

3. Respond to the voice by saying:

"I know this is what you think I am" (e.g., hopeless or power less), _____
"but I know I am" (e.g., strong and powerful), _____
_____.

4. Repeat this process every time the voice appears until you've conquered it.

As illustrated by Jimmy's example, we can acknowledge our thoughts and emotions without judgment, allowing them to simply exist.

PART 4

CHAPTER ELEVEN:

UNCONCIOUS THOUGHTS

The thoughts we frequently have become automatic and happen without us consciously realizing it. Over time, this repetition strengthens certain patterns in our brain, which can shape how we perceive reality.

As we explore how unconscious thoughts shape our perception through repetition, it becomes clear that the way we think day after day has a profound impact on our beliefs and view of reality. This concept aligns with the insights shared by Dr. Joe Dispenza.

Dr. Joe Dispenza on: How to Brainwash Yourself for Success & Destroy Negative Thoughts! In this podcast, Dr. Joe Dispenza shared profound insights during his talk as the featured speaker.

He emphasized that our thoughts tend to follow familiar patterns, with about 90% of our thinking mirroring the thoughts from the previous day.

He explained that repetitive thoughts eventually transform into beliefs, while our brain's nerve cells strengthen their connections t

hrough consistent firing.

These automatic connections make our thoughts unconscious, often blurring the line between truth and our subjective perception. this refers to the process by which our repetitive thoughts become ingrained and automatic.

As our brain's neural connections strengthen through repetition, these thoughts become unconscious, meaning we may not be fully aware of them or consciously analyze them.

This unconscious nature of our thoughts can lead to a blurring of the line between what is objectively true and our own subjective perception or interpretation of reality.

Here's a breakdown of the key components:

1. "Unconscious nature of our thoughts":

This refers to the idea that a significant portion of our thinking happens automatically and outside of conscious awareness. We may not actively think about or analyze these thoughts.

2. "Blurring of the line":

This indicates that the distinction or boundary between two things becomes less clear or defined.

3. "Objectively true":

This refers to facts or information that exist independent of personal opinions or biases. Objective truth is based on verifiable evidence.

4. "Subjective perception or interpretation of reality":

This describes how we individually interpret or understand

the world based on our own unique perspectives, beliefs, and

experiences. Subjectivity acknowledges that different people may have different interpretations or perceptions of the same reality.

When the unconscious nature of our thoughts leads to a blurring of the line between what is objectively true and our own subjective perception or interpretation of reality, it means that our automatic and unconscious thoughts can influence how we perceive the world.

This influence makes it more challenging to separate objective truth from our subjective viewpoints or biases. In other words, our automatic thought patterns can shape our perception of truth, making it harder to distinguish between objective reality and our personal biases or beliefs.

This explains why Jimmy's approach will require some effort. Due to the challenge of distinguishing between reality and perception, it is important to pay close attention and focus on the thoughts that arise from our past experiences. Through this process, we can identify the beliefs that have been formed and currently impact our feelings of anxiety, stress, and other emotions.

Dr. Joe also highlighted that accepting and surrendering to a thought without analyzing it can perpetuate a cycle of repetitive choices, behaviors, experiences, and emotions.

I appreciate the way he expressed it when he said, 'Just because you have a thought, it doesn't necessarily mean it is true. If you have that thought and you accept it, you believe it, surrendering to it without analyzing it.'

Then, he added, 'that thought will lead to the same choice, which will lead to the same behavior, resulting in the same experience and producing the same emotion.

This same emotion then drives those very same thoughts... over time, our biology, circuitry, chemicals, hormones, and gene expression remain unchanged,' and then he noted that embracing change can lead to discomfort as it challenges these familiar patterns.

In simple terms, Dr. Joe is saying that when we accept a thought without questioning it, we may unknowingly trap ourselves in a cycle. This cycle involves repeating the same choices, behaviors, experiences, and emotions over and over again.

For example, if we have a negative thought and just accept it as true without examining it, we're more likely to make choices and act in ways that reinforce that thought. This pattern keeps us stuck in familiar emotions, like stress or frustration, because our mind and body are used to them.

Over time, this repetition affects our biology—our brain circuits, chemicals, and even gene expressions stay the same because we're not challenging our patterns.

Dr. Joe emphasizes that real change requires breaking these patterns, which can feel uncomfortable. Stepping out of our comfort zone and questioning these automatic thoughts is key to creating new experiences, emotions, and a different version of ourselves.

Jimmy's approach will require considerable effort on our part due to the dominance of our inner thoughts, which have become deeply ingrained in our brains.

By saying this, we are referring to the idea that our long-standing patterns of thinking have remained unchanged for a significant period. It will require of our active participation and unwavering commitment to challenge and rewire our established patterns of thinking.

With time, patience, and consistent effort, and by embracing new perspectives, beliefs, and attitudes, it is possible to reshape our internal mindset and transcend the limitations of our previous thinking.

We have the power to reshape our own environment and create a more fulfilling and empowering existence.

THE BRAIN'S
ADAPTABILITY TO EXPERIENCE

According to neuroscience, our brain is incredibly adaptable and has the ability to rewire itself based on our experiences. This process is known as neuroplasticity.

When we repeatedly engage in certain thought patterns or behaviors, the neural pathways associated with those patterns become strengthened and more efficient, making them the default mode of operation for our brain.

If your inner thoughts have been dominated by negative or unhelpful patterns, such as self-doubt, pessimism, or limiting beliefs, it can be challenging to break free from them.

The more entrenched these patterns are, the harder it may be to change them. This is because the neural pathways associated with these thoughts have become well-established and automatic.

However, it's important to note that neuroplasticity works both ways. Just as negative patterns can become deeply ingrained, positive patterns and healthier ways of thinking can also be developed.

By consciously engaging in new thoughts, behaviors, and perspectives, you can start creating new neural connections and weakening the old ones. While it may not be easy to break free from deeply wired thought patterns, it is certainly possible with effort, practice, and patience.

Techniques like cognitive-behavioral therapy, mindfulness, positive affirmations, and self-reflection can all contribute to rewiring your brain and cultivating a more positive and empowering mindset.

Remember, the brain's plasticity means that change is always possible, and with persistence, you can gradually transform your thought patterns and achieve personal growth and well-being.

While neuroplasticity highlights the brain's ability to adapt and change through repeated thoughts and behaviors, creating lasting transformation requires consistent effort. This is where the 21/90 rule comes into play.

THE 21/90 RULE

The 21/90 rule, also known as the "Habit Formation Rule," suggests that it takes roughly 21 days of consistent effort to form a new habit and about 90 days for it to become a more permanent lifestyle change.

While the concept of habit formation has been discussed by various experts over the years, the specific formulation of the 21/90 rule is often attributed to Dr. Maxwell Maltz, a plastic surgeon and author.

In his book "Psycho-Cybernetics," published in 1960, Dr. Maltz explored the idea of habit formation and personal transformation.

Although the 21/90 rule is widely cited, it's important to note that the timeline for habit formation can vary depending on the individual and the complexity of the habit being developed.

Therefore, the 21/90 rule aligns well with the idea that rewiring thought patterns or forming new habits requires time, patience, and repetition, which is consistent with the concept of neuroplasticity discussed earlier.

In Jimmy's case, if he remains dedicated to building new thought patterns and consistently applies the necessary techniques and approaches, he can expect to start seeing significant progress within the initial 21 days.

By continuing to reinforce these new patterns for a total of 90 days, they are more likely to become deeply ingrained and habitual.

Remember that building new patterns and transforming thoughts is a journey that requires ongoing effort, self-reflection, and adaptation.

The 21/90 rule serves as a general guideline, but individual experiences may vary. The key is to stay committed, patient, and persistent in practicing the new patterns to create lasting change.

With persistence and dedication in time we will be greater than our environment; we will rise above the circumstances and influences of our surroundings. We will transcend limitations imposed by external factors and strive for personal growth and development.

TO BE GREATER
THAN YOUR ENVIRONMNET MEANS

1. Self-belief and empowerment: Developing an unshakable confidence in your ability to rise above circumstances, no matter how challenging. It involves recognizing your worth and tapping into your potential to create positive change.

2. Mindset shift: Transforming how you perceive challenges by viewing them as opportunities for growth rather than insurmountable barriers. This perspective enables you to see possibilities that others might overlook.

3. Resilience and determination: Cultivating the inner strength to face adversity with courage and perseverance. Resilience means not just enduring hardships but using them as stepping stones toward achieving your goals.

4. Personal growth: Embracing a commitment to lifelong learning and self-discovery. Whether through acquiring new skills, reflecting on past experiences, or striving to become the best version of yourself, growth becomes a central focus.

5. Influence and leadership: Choosing to positively impact those around you by leading with integrity and inspiring others to see their potential. This could mean uplifting your community, advocating for change, or simply being a role model in your environment.

Being greater than your environment is about stepping beyond limitations. It signifies refusing to let your surroundings dictate who you are or what you can achieve. Instead, it is taking charge of your narrative, making intentional choices, and striving for excellence while remaining adaptable in the face of challenges.

Jimmy's journey exemplifies this transformation. As he continues to address his anxiety, he is no longer merely reacting to his environment—he is actively shaping it.

Instead of succumbing to his old, limiting thought patterns, Jimmy consciously pauses to reflect and reassess. Through these intentional shifts, Jimmy finds himself on a path of growth.

His ability to navigate uncomfortable emotions and circumstances fosters a sense of strength and autonomy. By creating new thought patterns, Jimmy redefines his reality, and his increasing sense of inner peace and happiness is a testament to the power of his transformation.

Now, let's turn our attention to another story—Mia's. Through her experiences, we'll explore what happens when the freedom to make choices is stripped away, revealing the profound impact of external circumstances on identity formation.

PART 4

5

DID YOU SHAPE YOUR ENVIRONMENT OR DID IT SHAPE YOU?

CHAPTER TWELVE: THE MIA STORY

So far, Lucy has provided insights into how beliefs form and shape the narratives we create about our lives. These core beliefs serve as the foundation for our identity, defining how we see ourselves and interact with the world. By adulthood, these beliefs have constructed a complex story that influences every aspect of our lives.

From Johnny, we learned how beliefs rooted in fear can prevent action, as illustrated by his declaration, "I will never ever..." Jimmy's story, in turn, demonstrated how deeply ingrained beliefs are often tied to pivotal moments of anxiety.

These beliefs, formed in response to specific experiences, remain stored in memory and are reawakened by triggers, influencing his present- day reactions and emotions.

Now, we turn to Mia's story. Through her experiences, we'll explore what happens when the luxury of choice is unavailable. Mia's struggles began early in life, highlighting how external circumstances and societal pressures can constrain a person's ability to make decisions and shape their identity.

At five years old, Mia was a playful, joyous child living with her father. However, her world began to shift when classmates mocked her appearance.

At first, Mia didn't understand their ridicule, but she eventually realized the stark difference between herself and the other girls. While they wore cute dresses, Mia arrived at school in baggy pants and T-shirts, resembling a boy more than a girl.

Hurt and confused, Mia asked her father for a dress, but he refused. Whether due to financial constraints or other reasons, her request was denied.

Meanwhile, the bullying escalated, isolating Mia further. Hurtful taunts labeled her as a boy, eroding her confidence and creating a deep sense of not belonging.

The teasing took a toll on Mia's self-image. One day, as she reflected on the cruel comments, a troubling thought emerged: "I am ugly." This self-criticism soon intensified: "I'm not just ugly; I'm the ugliest one in the school."

These thoughts became ingrained, shaping how Mia saw herself. Mia withdrew from her peers, avoiding school and play. She sought comfort in sleep, retreating to bed each day after school, sometimes skipping meals to escape her feelings of feeling ugly.

Her struggles were compounded by circumstances beyond her control. Her father's refusal to let her wear a dress denied her a simple way to fit in and express herself. At school, the relentless bullying shattered her confidence.

Meanwhile, her mother's absence left Mia without the maternal support she needed during this challenging time.

Mia's story is a poignant reminder of how external forces and internalized beliefs can limit our choices, shape our identity, and leave us feeling isolated and powerless.

WHEN CHOICES
ARE LIMITED AND VOICES UNHEARD

Life can often be harsh, particularly for young children who are still navigating the world around them. Our environment plays a significant role in shaping who we become, especially when choices are limited or unavailable.

Unfortunately, even the most innocent requests from children are sometimes overlooked or dismissed by their caregivers, who may have faced similar disregard in their own lives.

The weight of external influences becomes apparent as life imposes decisions upon us, whether it's the school system, authorities, or the pressures of peers. Growing up, it often feels like choice is not an option, as external forces take precedence over personal agency. These dynamics highlight the challenging nature of childhood and the importance of fostering environments where children's voices and choices are respected and valued.

As Mia grew older and reunited with her mother, she continued to carry her beliefs of feeling ugly. One day, while watching her mother gracefully put on makeup, Mia thought to herself, 'that looks pretty, maybe I can try it too.'

Driven by curiosity, Mia decided to explore the idea of enhancing her appearance and invited her cousin to join in the adventure. Excitedly, they entered her mother's room, where they discovered a treasure trove of makeup in an elegant case.

With giggles and smiles, they carefully experimented with different shades, brushes, and techniques, transforming their faces into vibrant canvases.

Admiring their newfound looks in the mirror, a sense of joy

filled the room. They exchanged laughter and expressions of delight, exclaiming, 'It's fun!'

As Mia and her cousin reached the peak of their playtime, completely engrossed in their joyous exploration, their delightful moment was interrupted as their mother walked into the room and noticed them wearing heels and makeup.

In that pivotal moment, a sense of unease washed over them as they noticed their mother's expression and demeanor, which appeared noticeably angry and stern. The sudden change in her mother's face and demeanor caused them to freeze, uncertain of how their playful activities would be received.

The situation triggered memories of limited choices, reminiscent of when she was told she couldn't wear a dress to school. In that moment, a familiar feeling resurfaced within her, as if her options were once again being restricted.

She immediately thought to herself, 'Oh no, I am not allowed to wear makeup.' Her tremor and discomfort worsened as her mother began questioning her motives for wearing makeup.

Her mother begins by scolding Mia, bombarding her with questions like, 'Why are you wearing makeup and heels? Do you think you're a grown-up?' She even makes comments insinuating, 'Are you dressing up for boys? Who are you trying to impress?'

To her, it's simply a fun and innocent activity shared with her cousin, considering that she frequently witnesses her mother wearing makeup on a daily basis. Mia, being a young girl who didn't fully comprehend the questions asked, finds herself at a loss for words.

In that moment, the mocking and ridicule from not only her mother but also her grandmother intensify her uncertainty, causing her to freeze.

Memories rush back of when she was bullied by other children at school, further reinforcing her belief of being ugly and feeling powerless. It engenders a sense of helplessness, as if she lacks control over her choices.

Mia is left in a state of confusion, believing that something is inherently wrong with her and that there is nothing she can do because there are no options but to surrender to what mother and grandma say.

So, after a few minutes, feeling both scorned and confused, she removes the makeup and takes off the heels.

In the depths of her despair, she even questions her own existence, engulfed by a haunting notion that she is merely a ghostly presence, she feels as if she is of no value, slowly vanishing into nothingness.

Mia's self-perception has shifted from viewing herself as beautiful and attractive to perceiving herself as unattractive, undesirable, and lacking in physical appeal.

In that very moment Mia decided that she is no longer pretty and accepted. She thinks she is ugly and unwanted. Not only that, but in her young mind, she has become nothing and a nobody. Mia will grow up believing she has to settle for less because she is not worthy of anything good. In her little mind, she says, "I am ugly, I am nothing."

As of now, Mia's actions will align with what she believes about herself— "I am ugly, unwanted, and nothing." And "I have no choice but to surrender to life's options."

Mia, Johnny, Jimmy, and Lucy have all come to realize how the influence of their environments has, at times, left them with limited choices, forcing them to adapt to imposed circumstances.

In moments of despair or confusion, individuals often form beliefs that become deeply ingrained. When triggered, these beliefs cause discomfort, leading to repetitive patterns of seeking comfort that, over time, turn into ingrained habits.

The narratives we create based on our interpretations of experiences shape how we see ourselves, relate to others, and approach life. However, these stories can sometimes obscure our true identity, causing us to view ourselves through the lens of our beliefs rather than embracing our authentic selves.

Before external influences shape our beliefs, our identity is pure and untainted, representing our innate potential, curiosity, creativity, kindness, and resilience.

Reconnecting with this core identity can be a powerful journey of self-realization and personal growth. By rediscovering who we truly are, we can gain self-awareness and redefine the stories we live by, fostering emotional, mental, and spiritual development.

THE BEFORE AND AFTER
OF
IDENTITY FORMATION

Before life's challenges and external circumstances shape us, our identity is pure, untainted, and full of potential. As children, we are often driven by curiosity and wonder, embracing the world with enthusiasm and imagination.

Our sense of self is rooted in the inherent qualities we possess—kindness, resilience, creativity, and joy. During this time, life feels simple and limitless, and we navigate the world with trust, unburdened by the weight of expectations, judgments, or self-doubt.

However, as we grow, life introduces challenges—unexpected circumstances, societal pressures, and emotional struggles—that begin to chip away at this pure identity. These experiences often leave us questioning who we are, as external influences mold our beliefs, attitudes, and behaviors.

Faced with difficult circumstances, we instinctively form beliefs to make sense of the world around us. These beliefs, though often created as coping mechanisms, become deeply ingrained in our minds.

Mia, Johnny, Jimmy, and Lucy's stories highlight how these beliefs take root. In moments of despair or confusion, the mind interprets events and creates narratives based on those interpretations.

These narratives, in turn, shape how we view ourselves, how we relate to others, and how we perceive the possibilities life holds.

Over time, this cycle of belief formation, triggered discomfort, and habitual coping behavior solidifies into patterns that influence the course of our lives.

For instance, before Mia faced bullying or Johnny experienced rejection, they likely saw themselves and the world as welcoming, kind, and full of opportunity. Their early identities were not weighed down by feelings of inadequacy or fear.

But as challenges arose, they began to internalize limiting beliefs about themselves, obscuring their core identity. These beliefs transformed their perspectives, creating a divide between their authentic selves and the distorted images they held of who they were.

The "after" stage, shaped by these external influences, often sees individuals carrying the weight of self-doubt, fear, and limiting stories. The pure identity they once had becomes buried under layers of false narratives and coping mechanisms.

The world, once bright and filled with potential, now appears dimmed by the lens of these beliefs. Relationships become filtered through suspicion or insecurity, and the freedom to express one's true self feels constrained by the fear of judgment or rejection.

Recognizing this transformation is the first step toward healing and growth. By reconnecting with their authentic identity—the core self that existed before these distortions—individuals can embark on a transformative journey of self-discovery.

This process allows them to unravel the false narratives, challenge limiting beliefs, and embrace their true essence. It is a path to reclaiming the curiosity, confidence, and joy they once possessed.

As we've seen through these stories, our beliefs and the narratives we create can profoundly shape our lives. Yet, they are not fixed. By understanding the process of belief formation and recognizing its impact, we open the door to transformation and the possibility of living authentically and freely.

Let's now take a closer look at the contrast between the "before" and "after" in the lives of Johnny, Mia, and Jimmy.

By examining their experiences, we can better understand how challenges and circumstances shaped their beliefs, behaviors, and sense of self.

THE JOHNNY
BEFORE AND AFTER

Before:

Johnny was a sweet and studious boy with a kind heart and a passion for learning. He approached his studies with enthusiasm and perseverance, always eager to expand his knowledge.

Beyond academics, Johnny's compassion shone in his interactions—whether helping a classmate, comforting a friend, or offering support to others, he consistently showed genuine care for those around him.

His kindness and dedication painted the picture of a boy with a bright future, focused on personal growth and making a positive impact. Until the moment of disappointment disrupted his path, shaking his confidence and altering his once optimistic outlook on life.

After:

Deep in Johnny's heart, the belief "I am not important" took hold, shaping his thoughts and diminishing his sense of self-worth. He constantly felt inadequate, despite his talents, and prioritized others' needs over his own, neglecting his well-being. This self-neglect drained his emotional and physical health.

Johnny hesitated to assert himself, fearing rejection and remaining silent, locked in self-doubt. He avoided attention, blending into the background to avoid validating his belief in his insignificance. Opportunities for growth passed by, as his fear of failure kept him captive.

Seeking external validation for reassurance, he found fleeting comfort, but it never filled the void within.

However, a spark of hope emerged. Johnny began to realize that his limiting belief was not absolute. Encouraged by kind souls who saw his worth, he embarked on a journey of self- discovery, challenging the belief that had confined him. Slowly, he nurtured self-esteem, embraced his uniqueness, and learned to balance his needs with others'.

With newfound courage, Johnny asserted himself, recognizing the power of his voice and the significance of his contributions. Stepping out of the shadows, he embraced opportunities, understanding that even small actions could create meaningful change. As confidence grew, he found validation from within and embraced self-acceptance.

Though disappointment once overshadowed his qualities, Johnny reclaimed his identity through resilience and personal growth. By rediscovering his sweetness, studiousness, and kindness, he reintegrated these qualities into his life, allowing them to shine once more.

His journey demonstrates the power of transformation, proving that inherent worth and potential can always be reignited.

THE JIMMY
BEFORE AND AFTER

Before:
Jimmy was a joyful and curious little boy who radiated warmth and kindness. He had an adventurous spirit, always eager to explore the world around him. Whether it was climbing trees, solving puzzles, or building forts, Jimmy's days were filled with creativity and wonder.

He had a natural ability to connect with others, making friends effortlessly with his playful and generous nature. Jimmy was the kind of child who shared his toys without hesitation and looked out for his peers, often stepping in to cheer them up when they felt down.

At home, Jimmy was a source of light. He loved helping his mother with chores, cracking jokes to make her laugh, and listening attentively as she told stories. His inquisitive mind led him to ask endless questions, sparking lively conversations about everything from the stars in the sky to the purpose of ants in the garden.

Jimmy's inner world was filled with dreams of greatness, believing he could grow up to become anything he set his heart on. He approached each day with optimism, his laughter echoing in the air, a reminder of the innocence and boundless potential that defined him before misfortune struck.

After:
From a young age, Jimmy grappled with anxiety, often triggered by social situations where he felt pressured to be liked and accepted. These moments intensified his unease, creating a cycle of anxious thoughts and physical discomfort.

One day, at a large gathering with unfamiliar faces, Jimmy's anxiety surged—his heart raced, palms sweated, and dread consumed him. Thoughts of being judged or rejected flooded his mind, reinforcing his fears.

Determined to understand and overcome his anxiety, Jimmy embarked on a journey of self-discovery. Through reflection and therapy, he unearthed a deep-rooted belief that he needed to be perfect to be valued.

Shaped by past criticisms and feelings of being overlooked, this belief had fueled his anxiety. With newfound awareness, Jimmy recognized its limiting nature and began challenging it.

Step by step, Jimmy embraced self-compassion and let go of perfectionistic tendencies. He learned he didn't need to be flawless to be worthy of love and acceptance. With support and encouragement, he practiced coping strategies like deep breathing and grounding techniques, gradually developing healthier habits.

Over time, Jimmy redefined his identity, realizing his worth wasn't tied to external validation. Although anxiety still appeared occasionally, he no longer let it control him. He approached social situations with growing confidence and authenticity, proving to himself that he could navigate life on his own terms.

In summary, while disappointment had once restrained Jimmy's abilities, his inherent strength and resilience endured. Those qualities, though momentarily obscured, remained integral to his identity, waiting to shine again through his determination and growth.

THE MIA
BEFORE AND AFTER

Before:

Mia was a compassionate, sweet, and giving little girl. She possessed a natural inclination towards kindness and empathy, always considering the needs and feelings of others. Her compassionate nature extended to both humans and animals, as she had a tender heart that was eager to provide support and care.

Mia's sweetness was evident in her interactions with those around her. She radiated warmth and affection, offering genuine smiles and heartfelt gestures of love.

Her sweetness was infectious, brightening the lives of those who had the privilege of knowing her. Mia had a way of making others feel valued and cherished, as she believed in the power of love and connection.

Not only was Mia compassionate and sweet, but she was also filled with joy and happiness. She had a contagious zest for life, finding delight in even the simplest of things.

Mia's laughter was like music, echoing through the air and

spreading happiness to those who heard it. Her genuine joy uplifted the spirits of those around her, creating a positive and cheerful atmosphere wherever she went.

She was always ready to lend a helping hand, whether it was assisting a friend with homework, sharing her toys, or comforting someone in need. Mia's giving nature reflected a selflessness beyond her years, as she genuinely found fulfillment in being of service to others.

In summary, Mia embodied the qualities of compassion, sweetness, joy, and a heart of service. Her presence brought comfort, love, and happiness to those around her. Mia's innate goodness and readiness to serve made her a shining example of kindness, compassion and generosity. Until....

After:

Despite her vibrant nature, Mia found herself trapped in a suffocating web of confusion and despair. A deep sense of inadequacy consumed her, whispering that something was inherently wrong with her. It was as if a heavy cloud of self-doubt loomed over her, casting a shadow on her once sparkling spirit.

Mia's mother and grandmother, unknowingly, played a role in perpetuating her inner turmoil. Their judgments and expectations became shackles that confined her, leaving her convinced that surrender was her only choice. With a heavy heart, Mia accepted this fate, believing that she had no other options but to conform to their views.

One day, in a moment of desperation, Mia stood before the mirror. She hesitantly wiped away the layers of makeup that concealed her true self, feeling the weight of her false identity being stripped away.

The reflection that stared back at her was unfamiliar and fragmented. It was in this vulnerable state that Mia questioned her very existence, feeling like a mere specter fading into the void.

The belief of being unattractive and undesirable gripped Mia's heart, its relentless grip squeezing tighter with each passing day. The whispers of her unworthiness echoed in her mind, and she could no longer ignore the cruel verdict she had passed upon herself.

In her young and impressionable mind, Mia came to believe that she was nothing more than a faceless shadow in the crowd, destined to settle for less than she deserved.

The words "I am ugly" and "I am nothing" became an incessant refrain, seeping into Mia's thoughts and dictating her every action. They carved deep grooves in her perception of herself and the world around her.

As time went on, the vibrant colors of her world turned bleak, and hope seemed like a distant memory. The light within her flickered, threatening to fade away entirely.

However, little did Mia know that even in her darkest moments, a flicker of resilience still burned within her. Deep down, there was a glimmer of strength that longed to break free from the chains of self-doubt. Mia's journey to reclaim her true identity and rewrite her story had only just begun.

So, while the mocking and scorning limited Mia's expression of her positive qualities, it does not diminish the fact that those qualities still reside within her. They may be temporarily overshadowed or dormant, but with time, healing, and a renewed sense of purpose, Mia has the potential to rediscover and reignite those inherent qualities that made her who he was.

As Mia embarked on her quest for self-discovery, she would encounter unexpected allies and discover the transformative power of self-love and acceptance.

Through the guidance of mentors and the support of kindred spirits, Mia would gradually learn to challenge the beliefs that held her captive and embrace her inherent worthiness.

It wouldn't be an easy journey, for the echoes of "I am ugly" and "I am nothing" would linger. Yet, as Mia slowly unraveled the layers of

PART 5

self-doubt, she would uncover a truth far more beautiful than she could have ever imagined.

She would realize that her worth extended far beyond superficial appearances, and her value as a person went far deeper than any judgment passed upon her.

Johnny's, Jimmy's and Mia's journey serves as a reminder to us all that even in the darkest of times, the spark of resilience within us can guide us towards a brighter path.

As we embark on our own journeys of self-discovery, may we find the strength to challenge the beliefs that confine us and embrace our true worth, for it is within us all to create a story filled with authenticity, love, and boundless possibilities.

By piecing together, the story of how these beliefs shaped their identities, they now realize that they have the power to choose who they want to be. They can differentiate between beliefs perceived and beliefs intentionally created.

They can construct a new story for themselves, one that is personally chosen rather than dictated by the environment. In their journey of growth, the environment once made choices for them, but now they can consciously choose their beliefs.

They can opt for habits that are intentionally created rather than ones forced upon them. Consequently, they will no longer find themselves trapped in a state of helplessness; they will have the freedom to make choices.

Ultimately, they will never despair over something when they have options available to them. But the question is, how will they go about constructing a new story?

Lucy will now demonstrate how she will construct a new story about herself, others, and the world.

CHAPTER THIRTEEN:

UNCOVERING THE TRIGGERS
LUCY'S JOURNEY

Feeling overwhelmed, embarrassment floods Lucy's body—she experiences a tingling sensation in her stomach, and her mind becomes foggy, clouding her thoughts.

In her imagination, she sees others mocking her and perceiving her as unintelligent. Determined to understand the cause of her emotional reactions, Lucy realized she needed to uncover the triggers behind these intense feelings.

Although she knew it wouldn't be easy, she firmly believed that "where there's a will, there's a way." She began her journey by embracing moments of discomfort, welcoming them instead of avoiding them.

By facing these uncomfortable moments head-on, she hoped to identify the triggers that stirred up her emotions. Lucy was committed to stepping outside her comfort zone. Now, let's hear from Lucy as she shares her insights on how she achieved this transformation.

As Lucy transitions into adulthood, the challenges in her life have only grown, along with a noticeable increase in stress and anxiety.

She often wonders why she feels trapped in a never- ending cycle, with no relief.

Stress, anxiety, overwhelm, and unhappiness become persistent themes in her daily life. In one of her lowest moments, Lucy receives an unexpected call from her friend, Marcela.

With genuine concern, Marcela says, "Lucy, I know what you've been going through. My friend Johnny recently attended a workshop that changed his life. He learned valuable insights about his struggles, especially about weight gain, and he managed to lose it effortlessly. Maybe it could help you too."

Marcela's words immediately capture Lucy's attention. "While my weight is a concern, it's not my biggest worry," Lucy thought. "What truly troubles me is the constant unhappiness and misery that overshadow my life.

I keep asking myself if there's a way out of this emotional storm." Motivated by this hope, Lucy decided to attend the workshop, a question--and--answer method of training being offered as a way to discover what is behind the stirred--up emotions that overshadow her life and make her unhappy.

Q & A METHOD —
WHAT JUST HAPPENED?

During the sesison on Sunday morning, Lucy felt confident and ready to participate in a workshop. When the speaker chose her to share her thoughts, she raised her hand with enthusiasm.

However, as she began speaking into the microphone, her mind went blank. Frustrated and embarrassed, she stumbled over her words, uttering random phrases. "What just happened?"

Overwhelmed by embarrassment, Lucy experienced physical sensations like tingling in her stomach and a foggy mind. She imagined others mocking her, perceiving her as unintelligent and unable to express herself.

This embarrassment prompted her to withdraw, seeking solace in isolation. At home, she coped by binge-eating for comfort, wrapping herself in a blanket, and sleeping to suppress her emotions.

Let us analyze what disrupted Lucy's confidence and clouded her thinking.

1. Initial State: Lucy was confident and ready to participate.

2. Trigger Timeframe: The shift occurred between the moment the speaker called on her and when the microphone reached her.

3. Trigger Identification: Something in this brief period trig gered emotions that disrupted her confidence.

Using the question-and-answer method, we can help Lucy identify the thought or event that caused this change:

• Q: What was Lucy's initial state?
A: Ready and confident to participate.

• Q: When did the emotions arise?
A: Between being called on and speaking into the microphone.

• Q: What are we looking for?
A: A thought or trigger that caused the interruption.

By analyzing the context and asking these questions, Lucy can uncover what disrupted her confidence and work toward resolving it. So, what triggered Lucy's emotions and clouded her thinking? To un-cover this, we need to ask her directly:

"Lucy, what just happened?" — we need to trace it back to a past experience because present discomforts often stem from past events. Let's explore the story behind Lucy's emotions and uncover their source.

LUCY
RECOUNTING HER STORY

Lucy recalls a moment from her childhood when neighbors would visit and greet her with a friendly "hello." However, she would remain silent and not respond. The neighbors, puzzled, would glance at her mother and siblings, who would shrug, equally unsure why she didn't reply.

Then, someone would often remark, "She doesn't talk; the cat got her tongue." This situation happened repeatedly. At first, Lucy didn't understand the meaning of those words, so she paid little attention. However, as the remark persisted, she began to reflect on its meaning.

One day, she heard the phrase again, but this time, it echoed loudly in her mind. In that moment, Lucy internalized the phrase "She doesn't talk," attaching a negative perception to it. The potential judgment associated with not speaking stirred a mix of emotions within her, ranging from confusion to feelings of inadequacy and self-doubt.

The unexpected comment, "She doesn't talk; the cat got her tongue," hit Lucy like an icy shower on a winter day, shaking her confidence and leaving her deeply embarrassed. In that frozen moment, Lucy's mind tried to make sense of the phrase.

Though it would take years for her to fully understand its lasting impact, the comment planted a seed of doubt. Her internal dialogue echoed, "I am dumb, I cannot speak," reinforcing a belief that she lacked the ability to express her thoughts effectively.

This interpretation of the phrase profoundly shaped Lucy's self-perception and communication skills. The repeated remark, "She doesn't talk; the cat's got her tongue," solidified her belief that she was incapable of expressing her thoughts correctly. This became a core trigger for her self- doubt, leading her to avoid communication out of fear of judgment.

Follow-up Questions to Explore the Situation:

• Q: What is Lucy's interpretation of the phrase 'she doesn't talk; the cat got her tongue'?
A: "I don't know how to talk; I must be dumb."

• Q: What is an interpretation of something?
A: It is an opinion, a point of view, a perception, or a belief.

• Q: How did the repeated use of the phrase 'she doesn't talk; the cat got her tongue' shape her self-perception?
A: She concluded, "I do not know how to convey or express thoughts."

• Q: For emphasis, what phrase prompted her belief that 'I do not know how to express correctly'?
A: "She doesn't talk; the cat got her tongue."

When these events occurred, Lucy was just a young child, and her understanding of words and phrases was still developing. Over time, she internalized the idea that people were implying she lacked the ability to speak or express herself correctly. This belief became ingrained in her memory and shaped her sense of self.

Why did this have such a strong effect on Lucy? When someone suggests that you don't know how to communicate effectively, it can cause self-doubt about your abilities and skills.

In Lucy's case, she began to doubt her ability to convey thoughts clearly. This self-doubt threw her off balance, leading her to constantly question herself and set high expectations for how she should speak and express her thoughts. Her fear of judgment made her repeatedly ask herself, "Am I saying it right?" or "Am I meeting their expectations?"

The trigger, then, is not just about whether she's saying things correctly; it's the pressure she puts on herself to meet perceived expectations. She worries that others will judge her if she doesn't meet these standards. Interesting, isn't it?

As a result, Lucy was constantly asking, "Am I saying it right?" Similarly, in other situations, one might find themselves questioning, "Am I doing it right?"

This new understanding of herself reveals why, as an adult, Lucy unconsciously struggles to communicate her thoughts effectively. The persistent question, "Am I saying it right?" echoes in her mind as she prepares to speak, leading to stuttering and random statements whenever she is triggered.

This internal pressure and self-doubt hinder her ability to articulate clearly and confidently, clouding her mind at the moment she begins to speak.

Let's continue with the question-and-answer method to explore further. Our next question is, was Lucy able to identify the trigger?

• Q: What is the trigger in Lucy's case?
A: It might seem like it's the question, "Am I saying it right?" But that's not the core trigger.

This isn't the first time Lucy has expressed doubt with the question, "Am I saying it right?" It's happened many times before. Each time, she perceives that people are watching, ready to judge her—whether or not that judgment actually occurs. The mere sight of others around her stirs something deep within.

What is it? Could it be... fear? The fear of being judged? She clings to the belief that judgment is inevitable... but is it?

Remember, this isn't the first time Lucy has questioned herself with, "Am I saying it right?" Time and again, she perceives silent judgment from others, even if it never actually happens. The mere presence of people triggers her deep-seated fear of judgment, leading to anticipation and self-doubt.

Therefore, the true trigger is the presence of people whenever she is about to speak—a situation that occurs every time.

REVISIT
THE WORKSHOP

Now, let's revisit the 'WHAT JUST HAPPENED' moment at the workshop. Lucy did participate in giving her comment, but remember, she started to stutter, tremble, and ended up saying random things. How do you think she felt after this?

• Q: For emphasis, how did she feel after she was done giving her comment?
A: Of course, she was embarrassed.

• Q: How does the feeling of embarrassment make her feel?
A: Uncomfortable.

Uncomfortable is a feeling of unease, physical or emotional distress, or a lack of comfort. It can be triggered by anxiety or self-doubt and is both a physical and emotional sensation.

In Lucy's case, the mere presence of people—her trigger—sets off this emotional discomfort even before she speaks. She starts to feel nervous, her hands shake, and her voice falters. These are clear body sensations that reflect her internal emotional state.

Why does Lucy experience such unease before she even raises her hand to participate? Because she is already anticipating what might happen based on her perception, not reality.

Her mind is caught up in the fear that she might embarrass herself, rooted in the belief that she is not capable of expressing herself correctly. The mere presence of people intensifies this anticipation, making the situation even more overwhelming for her.

Anticipation is the act of mentally preparing for potential future events. In Lucy's case, she unconsciously imagines scenarios where she will say something wrong, triggered by the mere presence of people and her underlying belief that "I'm dumb, and I can't say things the right way."

This belief drives her expectation of failure, leading to feelings of anxiety and discomfort before she even begins to speak.

Whenever Lucy is around people, it triggers a recurring thought in her mind: "Am I saying it right?" This thought causes her to doubt herself and worry that others might judge her.

As a result, she becomes anxious and unsure about speaking, fearing that she will make a mistake or be criticized. Therefore, the presence of others heightens her self- doubt and intensifies her fear of judgment.

• Q: What prompts Lucy to anticipate?
A: The trigger: The mere presence of people.

• Q: What outcome is Lucy anticipating?
A: She anticipates that she will say something incorrectly, leading others to make fun of her, judge her, or assess her negatively.

• Q: Why is she anticipating that?
A: Because she doubts herself and constantly questions her ability to express herself.

This pattern originated in childhood when someone said, "She doesn't talk; the cat got her tongue." This remark solidified her belief that she couldn't communicate effectively. The mere presence of people continues to trigger that deep-seated self-doubt and fear of judgment.

Ultimately, behind these triggers lies a deeply rooted belief that drives Lucy's reactions: "I'm dumb, and I can't say things the right way."

This belief shapes her anticipation, emotions, and physical sensations. As soon as she is prompted to speak, the mere presence of people—the trigger—sets off a cascade of emotions: fear, anxiety, and ultimately, embarrassment, all reinforced by the anticipation of judgment from others.

CHAIN OF EVENTS

• Trigger:
The initial spark that sets off the chain, such as "the mere presence of people" when Lucy is prompted to speak. This situation initiates a cascade of internal reactions.

• Belief:
A deep-seated conviction that surfaces because of the trigger. In Lucy's case, the belief is "I can't say things the right way."

This belief colors how she perceives herself and the situation. •

• Emotions:
The feelings that arise from the belief. For Lucy, emotions like fear, anxiety, and self-doubt are triggered, making her feel overwhelmed and vulnerable.

• Defense Mechanism:
The way Lucy instinctively protects herself from these painful emotions. She may stumble over words, withdraw, or avoid speaking to shield herself from perceived judgment.

• The Cycle:
This repeating pattern where the defense mechanism reinforces the belief, which, in turn, makes Lucy more sensitive to the trigger. Each time the trigger appears, the cycle begins again, keeping her stuck in a loop of self-doubt and fear.

Now that Lucy has identified the trigger, she stands at a crossroads. She understands what's happening inside her mind and body and faces a crucial choice: she can either hold onto the trigger and belief, letting them control her emotions, or she can choose to release them. The challenge is how to let go of a belief that has influenced her for so long.

Lucy now sees the chain reaction clearly: (1) the trigger sparks a belief, (2) leading to overwhelming emotions and (3) defensive reactions.

This cycle keeps her trapped in self-doubt and fear. She now has the chance to break free—either remain stuck or let go.

The question is, how can Lucy effectively let go of the trigger? What steps can she take to break the cycle? Before diving into strategies, pause and reflect on your own situation. Consider a challenge you're facing and identify the trigger behind it. The following is a guide to help.

STEPS TO
IDENTIFYING YOUR TRIGGER

1. Describe your current situation: What are you dealing with right now?

2. Narrow it down:
Focus on one specific area of your life (e.g., relationships, self-expression, family dynamics,
health, etc.).

3. Reflect on your state of mind:
How did you feel right before experiencing a 'what just happened' moment?

4. Identify the time frame:

Look at the period between when your state of mind was calm or neutral and the moment emotions became stirred up. Once you pinpoint this timeframe, you can more easily identify what triggered the change in your emotions.

This process clarifies how Lucy's trigger leads to the belief, how that belief evokes intense emotions, and how those emotions prompt a defensive reaction, perpetuating a repeating cycle.

By recognizing this, Lucy can begin taking steps to break free from the cycle.

• Q: So, what are we looking for at this point?
A: We are looking for a cause or a trigger.

To identify the trigger(s), it is crucial to acknowledge that most discomforts in the present have a story rooted in our past experiences. With that in mind, let's delve into the question: What is the story behind these discomforts?

STORY
BEHIND THE DISCOMFORT

In that frozen state, Lucy internalized the idea, "I am dumb; I cannot speak." This belief was triggered by an unexpected comment: "She doesn't talk; the cat's got her tongue." That remark left a lasting impact on her perception of herself and her communication skills.

Over time, Lucy's fear of judgment, lack of confidence, and social anxiety began to surface in similar situations, driven by the belief that she couldn't express herself effectively.

For Lucy, the presence of people became a powerful trigger, activating her belief that others were silently judging her, even without evidence.

This belief often brought about a physical response—tension, a racing heart, or a dry mouth—and an emotional response rooted in the fear of being judged.

These patterns created a cycle where the physical sensations and emotional reactions reinforced the belief, making Lucy doubt herself even more.

The words, "She doesn't talk; the cat got her tongue," became deeply ingrained in her mind, leading her to constantly question, "Am I saying it right?"

Some common causes of discomfort that may apply to Lucy's experience include:

1. Fear of judgment   2. Lack of confidence   3. Social anxiety
4. Previous negative experiences   5. Perfectionism

Ask yourself: What words or phrases trigger your discomfort?

Below are some common factors that contribute to feelings of unease:

1. Uncertainty or ambiguity
2. Fear or anxiety
3. Change or transitions
4. Conflict or disagreement
5. Unmet expectations
6. Feeling overwhelmed or overloaded
7. Perceived threats or danger
 8. Social or performance pressure
9. Feeling judged or criticized
10. Loss or grief
11. Feeling out of control
12. Guilt or shame
13. Injustice or unfair treatment
14. Past traumatic experiences
15. Personal insecurities or self-doubt

These patterns illustrate how triggers can activate beliefs, which in turn lead to emotional and physical responses. In Lucy's case, the trigger—being surrounded by people—activated her belief that she was being silently judged. This belief then stirred up a physical sensation of anxiety, manifesting as a racing heart and tension.

The emotional response—fear of being judged—followed. Together, these responses reinforced Lucy's self-doubt and heightened her fear of expressing herself.

The repeated childhood phrase, "She can't talk; the cat got her tongue," left her caught in a loop of self-doubt and the constant worry of whether she was expressing herself correctly.

What will Lucy do to break free from this cycle and rebuild her confidence? Before exploring this question, let's turn to Johnny and see how he overcomes his own challenges.

JOHNNY'S
STORY CONTINUED

Johnny realized he needed to rise above his environment and focus on internal factors influencing his behavior.

After years of battling his weight through dieting, eating less, and exercising more, he noticed the results were always temporary. Inspired by Mia's introspection, Johnny decided to investigate the internal triggers that led to his binge-eating habits.

He embraced moments of discomfort, recognizing them as opportunities to uncover the root causes of his behavior. Johnny said, "I worked on my weight for years, but external factors like dieting and exercise weren't enough. I realized I needed to address the internal issues—the thoughts and beliefs that drove my eating habits.

By observing my environment and emotions, I began identifying the triggers tied to my self-image and past experiences. This process helped me uncover why I overeat and allowed me to take control."

Johnny started by paying attention to his present surroundings and how they affected his emotions. He observed his thoughts, feelings, and actions before turning to food for comfort. For example, at the law firm where Johnny works, the demanding tasks and constant pressure often leave him feeling overwhelmed.

When his boss approaches him with questions about unfinished reports, Johnny feels anxious and self-conscious. As soon as his boss leaves, he reaches for food to soothe the discomfort.

Analyzing the Sequence:

1. Morning Mood: Johnny arrives at work feeling confident and ready to tackle his day.

2. Trigger Event: His boss approaches, asking about his progress on

reports.

3. Emotional Shift: Johnny begins doubting his abilities, imagining others perceive him as
incapable.

4. Response: Overwhelmed by these thoughts, Johnny reaches for food to soothe his discomfort.

By identifying this pattern, Johnny can pinpoint the exact moment his emotions shift and address the underlying belief driving his behavior. In this case, the belief is tied to a fear of failure and judgment, which leads him to self-soothe with food.

Johnny understands that these triggers are rooted in a past decision he made about himself. By addressing this belief and practicing self-awareness, he begins to reclaim control over his emotions.

Rather than reaching for food, he pauses to question the thoughts causing his discomfort, allowing him to break the cycle and focus on healthier coping mechanisms.

IN THE
PRESENT MOMENT

Johnny is working to identify the internal factors behind his unnecessary eating and bingeing. By observing his surroundings, emotions, and thoughts before reaching for food, he aims to uncover the triggers that lead to these behaviors.

Johnny works at a law firm, where the demanding workload often leaves him feeling overwhelmed. Negative thoughts creep in, imagining others judging him as unintelligent or incapable.

These feelings of failure and inadequacy lead him to reach into his backpack for food to soothe his discomfort. This pattern repeats, contributing to recurrent weight gain. At home, he copes by binge eating, further affecting his well-being.

Sequence of Events:

Johnny begins the day feeling ready and confident. However, as the day progresses, his emotions shift. The turning point often occurs when his boss approaches, asks about his progress, and leaves. After this interaction, Johnny feels discomfort and immediately turns to food.

What Just Happened?

To pinpoint the trigger, consider the timeframe:

• Q: What was Johnny's emotional state at the start of the day?
A: He was ready and confident until his boss spoke to him.

• Q: What is the timeframe for the emotional shift?
A: Between his boss's approach and departure.

The boss's presence and inquiry seem to activate Johnny's discomfort.

Now, to uncover the specific trigger:

• Q: What are we looking for?
A: The thought or belief tied to his emotional reaction.

The root cause lies in Johnny's internal dialogue—what he tells himself when his boss interacts with him. This thought process prompts feelings of inadequacy, leading him to seek comfort through food.

JOHNNY
WHAT JUST HAPPENED? —
TRACING IT BACK (past experience)

The first thing that comes to mind for Johnny is a time when he returned home from school and discovered that his parents had met with his teacher to discuss his dropping grades.

PART 5

As Johnny arrives home after the conference, his father confronts him at the door, expressing disappointment and treating him as if he were an adult. His father demands an explanation for Johnny's reported failing grades.

This incident comes to mind every time Johnny's boss approaches him at work. In that moment, Johnny is reminded of his father's words, and it affects him emotionally.

Fifteen years have passed since his father said to him, "Johnny, listen carefully. Education is the foundation of success in life, and I need you to understand its significance. If you don't put your heart into your studies, it could have serious consequences.

A lackluster education may lead you down a path to failure, I worry about how people might perceive you. I care about your future, and I want you to achieve greatness. So, I urge you to take your education seriously and give it your all."

So, every time his boss approaches, his mind transports to that time in his life. Now the question is, 'when Johnny sees his boss coming, what do you think he's thinking?'

"Oh no, here he comes, and he's going to ask for an explanation, just like my father used to." In that moment, Johnny's heart starts racing, and his mind replays the words his father once said about the significance of education and the fear of being seen as a failure. These thoughts add to the pressure he feels when facing his boss, making him question his abilities and competence.

The fear of disappointing his boss and being labeled a loser intensifies, creating a sense of unease and anxiety within Johnny. So, can you see what it is that creates the unease that triggers him to eat and binge?

• Q: What is the trigger?
A: Oh no, here he comes, and he's going to ask for an explanation, just like my father used to.

It might seem like that thought triggers the commotion, but it's not. I'll give you a hint: it happens right before Johnny notices his boss coming or immediately after his boss appears in his presence.

So, it's not the environment in the office, it's not his coworkers, and it's not the space he occupies. Then what is it? Think about this: which of his antennas (his senses) is at work in this moment to alert Johnny of approaching danger? Could it be his boss's presence?

• Q: What is the trigger? A: It is his boss's presence.

That's it. Consider the time frame when the commotion happens. It occurs between him being okay until he sees or hears the steps of his boss approaching. This specific moment is what alters Johnny's emotions.

So, what is it that really triggers Johnny? With the context provided, it seems that his boss's presence, or the anticipation of his boss's arrival, is the primary trigger for the unease and emotional turmoil he experiences.

The mere sight or sound of his boss seems to activate a deep emotional response, likely tied to his past experiences and feelings of inadequacy.

Johnny's fear of his boss's presence is likely rooted in his concern that he will be perceived as a failure and a loser due to his struggles with completing work on time.

The pressure to meet expectations and the fear of disappointing his boss may intensify his unease and trigger emotions related to his self-image and past experiences.

Johnny's past association of being seen as a loser if he doesn't excel in his education might have extended to his work life, leading to a deep-seated fear of not meeting expectations and facing the consequences of failure.

As a result, whenever his boss approaches, these insecurities resurface, and he becomes apprehensive about his abilities, fearing the judgment of others.

When tracing it back to his past, what his father said when Johnny was 5 or 6 years old is, 'Education is the foundation of success. If you don't put your heart into your studies, it could have serious consequences.

A lackluster education may lead you down a path to failure, I worry about how people might perceive you. So, I urge you to take your education seriously and give it your all.' But what Johnny heard was: 'If you don't take education seriously, you will be a failure and an underachiever.'

Johnny's interpretation of his father's words has led to his fear of failure and the pressure he feels when facing authority figures, like his boss. So, when Johnny sees his boss approaching, he is triggered. The presence of his boss is the trigger.

Now, let us answer the question: what does the boss's presence trigger? It triggers a story he has about authority figures, and that story is: 'If you don't take education seriously, you might end up as a failure and an underachiever, and my father will be disappointed.

Similarly, if you don't complete your assignments on time, you could risk getting fired and be seen as unsuccessful, and your boss will be disappointed.'

So, what weighed on him most was the fear of disappointing his father. Likewise, the prospect of getting fired and being seen as unsuccessful could induce feelings of insecurity and the need to constantly meet expectations. But above all, what troubled him the most was the worry of letting down his boss.

So, upon sensing his boss approach, he is present to, he will be disappointed. 'Oh no,' he thinks. This is what occupies his mind precisely at the moment.

Now, let's continue with the question-and-answer method. Our next question is, 'Was Johnny able to identify the trigger?'

• Q: What is the trigger in johnny's case?
A: The present of his boss.

When Johnny is at home, the thought of facing his boss the next day triggers anxiety, leading him to start eating. He anticipates disappointment from his boss due to unfinished reports.

However, this fear isn't grounded in reality—it's how Johnny perceives the situation. In truth, his boss might be patient and understanding, but Johnny views him as a looming threat.

The anxiety Johnny experiences stems from his own interpretations and fears, not his boss's actual behavior. Recognizing this misalignment, Johnny begins to understand that his anticipations are merely assumptions.

This realization prompts crucial questions: What is the origin of these anticipations? What underlying beliefs fuel them? Where did it all begin, and what belief lies at the root of these assumptions?

• Q: Where did it start, what is the belief behind all these assumptions?
Once Johnny delved deeper into understanding the root causes of his fears and anxieties, this answer is —
A: Johnny's assumptions and anxieties stem from believing that he is a failure and a disappointment.

So now Johnny will recreate these conversations. He will start by acknowledging and allowing his fears to be present rather than resisting them. By accepting their presence, he creates the mental space needed to challenge and reshape them.

Then, he will intentionally put in place a new anticipation. Instead of expecting criticism or disappointment, he will envision his boss approaching him with understanding and encouragement. For example, Johnny might imagine his boss saying, "Johnny, take your time. Good morning. The reports will get done because, being the person that you are, you will have them done on time," or something similar.

This mental rehearsal of positive interactions shifts Johnny's perspective. He is not changing his boss's behavior but altering his own perception of it. The key lies in cultivating a mindset that anticipates support rather than criticism.

However, Johnny understands that this transformation won't happen overnight. As Dr. Maxwell Maltz explains in Psycho-Cybernetics, it takes 21 days of consistent practice to dissolve an old mental image and replace it with a new one, and around 90 days for that new image to become a conviction.

With this knowledge, Johnny is committed to the process. Each day, he will reinforce the new anticipation, recognizing that repetition is crucial. By doing so, he gradually rewires his thinking, replacing fear with confidence and negativity with optimism.

This shift not only changes how Johnny perceives his boss but also empowers him to approach work with a renewed sense of control and self-assurance. By replacing his previous negative anticipation with a new, positive thought pattern and understanding, Johnny can work towards reshaping his perception and managing his anxieties effectively.

Steps Johnny Will Take to Regain Composure:

1. Recognize the Trigger:
• When his boss approaches or when he thinks about seeing him the next day, Johnny will acknowledge that the trigger is activated.

2. Acknowledge Thoughts and Feelings:
• He will write down or say out loud everything he's thinking or feeling, such as:
"Here he comes, and he's going to ask for the reports! He'll see me as a failure, and I'll feel anxious."

3. Repeat to Decrease Intensity:
• He will repeat these phrases until the intensity of his emotions begins to decrease.

4. Introduce a New Positive Thought:
• Without waiting for the thought to completely disappear, Johnny will introduce a new positive thought to shift his mindset.

5. Practice Visualization:
• He will practice visualizing his boss as understanding and patient, reinforcing this positive image in his mind.

6. Replace Old Thoughts When They Return:
• If the old thought returns, Johnny will acknowledge it, express it again, and consciously replace it with the new positive thought.

He will continue this process of repeating and replacing until the trigger no longer causes him anxiety, allowing him to work with a clear and distraction-free mind, focused on his tasks without fear.

So, in working with internal factors, the external factors followed. This means that by addressing and resolving issues related to one's internal thoughts, emotions, or beliefs, the external aspects of their life, such as actions, behaviors, or circumstances, tend to fall into place or improve accordingly.

In other words, when individuals work on their inner mindset, it often has a positive impact on their outer experiences and interactions with the external world.

It all boils down to an occurring world Johnny created when he was a little kid, and this has carried over to his adult life, as it just keeps recurring.

You can be sure this is not the first time he has experienced this cycle, the fears and anxieties from his past experiences with authority figures, particularly his father. Throughout his adult life, the recurring pattern has persisted, leading him to confront the same challenges repeatedly.

Despite attempts to break free from the deeply ingrained patterns, these past experiences seem to color his interactions with his boss and influence his emotional responses to the world.

By understanding and reshaping his occurring world, Johnny can gradually free himself from the burdens of the past and build a more positive and confident outlook on his present and future interactions.

Before his first encounter with disappointment, Johnny was smart and joyous, and the world felt like a safe place for him. Then, he faced his first disappointed and a few others thereafter, he started to create a world of turmoil within himself based all in his internal dialogue.

Despite his efforts to lose weight, he was getting the same results for years. Once he focused on INTERNAL FACTORS, to reshape his inner dialogues, Johnny was able to RECOVER his true identity, and achieve the intended results related to his ideal weight.

By working with internal factors, one can achieve any intended results and become who we choose to be, not someone shaped solely by the environment. Now, let's explore how Lucy will break free from the vicious cycle and rediscover her true identity.

LUCY STORY —
CONTINUED—THINK FROM, NOT OF

What will Lucy do to break free from the vicious cycle and build self-assurance while overcoming feelings of inadequacy?

Let's review the sequence of events: Lucy's anticipation of potential negative reactions during speaking leads to embarrassment, which, in turn, causes her to retreat to her comfort zone of eating and seeking solace by wrapping herself in a blanket before going to sleep.

• Q: What is Lucy's anticipation?
A: potential negative reactions from the audience during and after her participation.

Lucy will start by rerunning the mentally the story that was constructed at age probably between 5 and 6. She will invite situations that involve speaking, especially in public speaking to stir up the emotions; as they are pulled up she will review and write down everything that shows up, and then read it all in front of a mirror as she is speaking to that child that constructed the story.

She will do this until the anxiety becomes less and less, then she will start thinking from a different angle, she will practice THINKING FROM RATHER THAN THINK OF. As in think from a certain point, a certain place, a certain space. As in being inside a certain area or situation and thinking from there rather than thinking of.

In other words, she will create a new anticipation, she will choose an anticipation to think from rather that's thinking from the anticipation given by her past.

Example:
Old anticipation: potential negative reactions from the audience during and after her participation.

New anticipation: Everyone will applaud and congratulate me for my well-done participation.

So now is your turn— start by re-running the story that was created in your mind at a very young age.

_____
_____
_____
_____

Next, think of your old anticipation and write it down.

_____
_____
_____
_____

Then think of your new anticipation and write it down.

_____
_____

So, when Lucy began envisioning herself with the new anticipation, 'Everyone will applaud and congratulate me for my well-done participation,' she experienced ease and serenity.

The trigger that once affected her was no longer there, eliminating the need to seek a comfort zone through overeating, bingeing, or wrapping herself in a blanket, as she no longer required that level of comfort.

Additionally, by addressing the trigger and embracing the new anticipation, Lucy was able to reduce the feelings of embarrassment, stuttering, and mumbling while speaking. The need to hide under a metaphorical blanket and resort to unnecessary eating or binge-eating completely vanished from her life.

Interestingly, although weight loss was not her primary goal, it naturally occurred as a result of no longer being consumed by constant eating and binging.

This positive transformation allowed Lucy to break free from the coping mechanisms that once held her captive. Instead of seeking comfort through overeating or binge-eating, she found relief in her newfound self-confidence and ability to face situations with ease.

As she continued to reinforce this healthier mindset and approach to life, her relationships and interactions with others improved. The fear of judgment and the need for constant validation diminished, replaced by a newfound sense of self-assurance and empowerment.

Overall, Lucy's journey of self-discovery and growth serves as an inspiring reminder of the power that lies within us to overcome our struggles and reshape our lives for the better.

The identifying of triggers is quantifiably important for identifying emotions, feelings, beliefs and habits, TRIGGERS are THE SWITCHES THAT TURN ON THE commotion in OUR mind and body.

So how to identify triggers plays a huge role in you becoming a complete soul (meaning, in gaining back what you lost as a child) which is our happiness, our communication skills, our ability to love, your compassionate being, your humanity. And all that makes you a WHOLE, COMPLETE AND PERFECT HUMAN BEING.

In conclusion, life's journey often takes unexpected turns, and as children, we may experience shifts from happiness and joy to challenges and disappointment.

These early experiences shape our thoughts and perceptions, which can continue to impact us as adults. However, as we mature, we must recognize the importance of taking responsibility for our lives.

The memories and emotions from our past may linger, but we have the power to shape our present and future. It is up to us to confront these feelings and find healthy ways to cope with them. As adults, we carry the responsibility of nurturing ourselves emotionally and mentally.

By acknowledging our past and its influence, we can make conscious choices to improve our well-being and relationships. Each day presents an opportunity to grow, heal, and create a fulfilling life for ourselves.

Embracing this responsibility empowers us to face challenges with resilience and forge a path towards happiness and fulfillment. Let us remember that we hold the key to our own happiness, and it starts with taking ownership of our lives as responsible adults.

CONCLUSION
ON JOHNNY'S STORY

"So, now that I am an adult," Johnny said, "I must be responsible for my way of being. I must be responsible for how I treat myself and others. this is whom I have become, and I am now responsible for how i will conduct myself and how I treat others.

Just because I think people don't care about me, it does not mean that I am going to neglect, ignore and disregard their attitude towards me.

I will respond and act as if they truly like me, I do not know if they do or not, but I am not responsible for them; I am responsible for my behavior. And as an adult I will behave politely, likable and desirable. This is the message I want to send out, regardless of how people will respond.

CONCLUSION
ON LUCY'S STORY

"Now that I'm an adult," said Lucy, "I recognize that I am responsible for how I treat myself and others. Throughout my life, I've faced fears and doubts that made me feel small and voiceless. But I realize I don't have to stay trapped in that version of myself.

Now, I'm responsible for how I want to live and how I want to show up in the world. It doesn't matter if others judge me or not; I choose to act with confidence, empathy, and openness.

I want to send the message that I am someone who values herself and is ready to connect with others, without letting fear hold me back. Today, I choose to live authentically and be the best version of myself, regardless of how others respond."

THE EMOTIONAL MENU

PART 5

ABOUT THE AUTHOR

LUZ IS A DYNAMIC AND ACCOMPLISHED WOMAN WHOSE LIFE JOURNEY EXEMPLIFIES RESILIENCE, DETERMINATION, AND BOUNDLESS LOVE FOR HER FAMILY. BORN IN A SMALL TOWN, LUZ IMMIGRATED TO THE UNITED STATES AS A TEENAGER, DRIVEN BY A DREAM OF CREATING A BETTER FUTURE FOR HERSELF AND HER LOVED ONES. SETTLING IN ATLANTA, GEORGIA, SHE EMBRACED THE CHALLENGES OF A NEW CULTURE AND LANGUAGE WITH UNWAVERING COURAGE.

AS A SINGLE MOTHER TO FIVE CHILDREN, LUZ JUGGLED THE DEMANDS OF PARENTHOOD WHILE PURSUING HER ENTREPRENEURIAL AMBITIONS. OVER THE YEARS, SHE SUCCESSFULLY LAUNCHED AND MANAGED SEVERAL THRIVING BUSINESSES, RANGING FROM RETAIL TO HOSPITALITY, EARNING A REPUTATION AS A SHARP, INNOVATIVE BUSINESSWOMAN. HER VENTURES NOT ONLY SUPPORTED HER FAMILY BUT ALSO BECAME A SOURCE OF INSPIRATION FOR HER CHILDREN, WHO ADMIRED HER WORK ETHIC AND DETERMINATION TO SUCCEED AGAINST ALL ODDS.

DESPITE HER BUSY SCHEDULE, LUZ ALWAYS PRIORITIZED HER ROLE AS A MOTHER AND GRANDMOTHER. HER LOVE AND DEDICATION TO HER FAMILY ARE THE CORNERSTONES OF HER LIFE. TODAY, SHE DELIGHTS IN SPENDING TIME WITH HER EIGHT GRANDCHILDREN, SHARING STORIES OF HER JOURNEY AND IMPARTING WISDOM THAT STEMS FROM HER RICH EXPERIENCES.

LUZ'S LIFE IS A TESTAMENT TO HER RESILIENCE AND BELIEF IN THE POWER OF HARD WORK AND COMMUNITY. A PROUD ATLANTA RESIDENT, SHE ACTIVELY PARTICIPATES IN LOCAL ORGANIZATIONS THAT SUPPORT IMMIGRANT FAMILIES AND WOMEN ENTREPRENEURS, OFFERING MENTORSHIP AND GUIDANCE TO THOSE NAVIGATING CHALLENGES SIMILAR TO HER OWN. LUZ'S JOURNEY SERVES AS A REMINDER THAT WITH DETERMINATION, LOVE, AND VISION, ANYTHING IS POSSIBLE.

UNLOCK THE SECRETS HIDDEN IN THE REST OF THE SERIES

IF WHAT JUST HAPPENED CAPTIVATED YOU, THE JOURNEY DOESN'T END HERE.

DIVE DEEPER INTO THE WORLD OF MYSTERY, STRATEGY, AND DISCOVERY WITH THE REST OF THIS GROUNDBREAKING SERIES. EACH INSTALLMENT TAKES YOU FURTHER INTO THE INTRICACIES OF DECEPTION, TRUTH, AND EMPOWERMENT.

• BOOK TWO: UNRAVELING THE WEB OF DECEPTION

NAVIGATE A WORLD OF MISINFORMATION AND MASTER THE SKILLS NEEDED TO DISCERN FACT FROM FICTION.

• BOOK THREE: DECODING PUZZLING MOMENTS

EXPLORE THE ULTIMATE SHOWDOWN BETWEEN TRUTH AND DECEPTION, EQUIPPING YOURSELF WITH THE KNOWLEDGE TO RISE ABOVE THE CHAOS.

EVERY BOOK BUILDS UPON THE LAST, OFFERING A COMPREHENSIVE GUIDE TO SEEING THROUGH ILLUSIONS AND GAINING CLARITY IN AN INCREASINGLY COMPLEX WORLD.

JOIN THE THOUSANDS OF READERS WHO ARE UNLOCKING THE TRUTH—ONE BOOK AT A TIME.

COMPLETE YOUR COLLECTION TODAY!

FOR MORE GREAT FINDS VISIT

THEEMOTIONALMENU.COM

+

TO FOLLOW ALONG IN REAL TIME
FOLLOW US ON SOCIAL MEDIA!

YouTube: @theemotionalmenu
TikTok: @theemotionalmenu
Instagram: @theemotionalmenu
Facebook: Luz M. Vasquez
Instagram: @luz_m_vasquez
TikTok: @luz_m_vasquez
YouTube: @theemotionalmenu

www.ingramcontent.com/pod-product-compliance
Lightning Source LLC
Chambersburg PA
CBHW051140020726
47501CB00005B/1596